OTHER YEARLING BOOKS YOU WILL ENJOY

BILLY HOOTEN OWLBOY

The Girl with the Destructo Touch

by Thomas E. Sniegoski

illustrated by Eric Powell

A YEARLING BOOK

For Katie Mignola. A key to the city.

Published by Yearling, an imprint of Random House Children's Books
a division of Random House, Inc., New York

Visit us on the Web! www.randomhouse.com/kids

Educators and librarians, for a variety of teaching tools, visit us at
www.randomhouse.com/teachers

Library of Congress Cataloging-in-Publication Data
Sniegoski, Tom.
The girl with the destructo touch / by Thomas E. Sniegoski ; [illustrations by Eric Powell].
p. cm. — (Billy Hooten, Owlboy)
Summary: Billy Hooten's inquisitive, five-year-old neighbor inadvertently finds her way
to Monstros, the underground city where Billy fights crime as the superhero Owlboy,
and he must save her from the monstrous inhabitants.
ISBN 978-0-440-42181-8 (trade : alk. paper) — ISBN 978-0-385-90403-2 (lib. bdg. : alk. paper)
[1. Heroes—Fiction. 2. Monsters—Fiction.] I. Powell, Eric, ill. II. Title.
PZ7.S68033Gi 2007
[Fic]—dc22
2007001556

Printed in the United States of America

July 2007

10 9 8 7 6 5 4 3 2 1

CHAPTER 1

The stink was awful.

Billy wrinkled his nose in disgust, wishing his Owl-boy suit had come with a gas mask. "It really smells," he whispered into one of Archebold's pointy ears.

"What'd you expect? Roses?" the goblin asked with a shrug, keeping his eyes on the curve of the tunnel ahead. "It's the sewer."

Billy tried breathing through his mouth, but that only made it worse because now he could taste the stink. He started to gag.

"Shhhh!" Archebold ordered, placing a stubby, clawed finger to his lips. "They'll be here any minute."

Billy felt foolish. "Sorry," he said. He'd been at this

whole superhero thing for a few weeks now, and it was awesome. But every once in a while, something would happen to make him feel like just a kid in a costume—such as this trek into the Monstros City sewer system.

He pulled his legs up closer to his body where he and Archebold sat on the slimy stone ledge and peered down at the steady flow of sewage. There were things floating in the water that he couldn't identify, which he decided was probably for the best. The filthy water reminded him of what had brought them here in the first place.

Monstros City had been experiencing a wave of burglaries, and the police had run out of ideas.

It had looked like a job for Owlboy. But at the site of the most recent robbery, even Billy and Archebold had been stumped. All the doors and windows had been locked and the security system activated, yet the house had still been burgled. Even after going over the place with a fine-tooth comb, he and Archebold were completely dumbfounded.

It was at that point that Billy—nervous that his reputation as the newest Owlboy in the city of monsters might be tarnished—had had to use the bathroom wicked bad. And there he had found the clue that had led to their current, fragrant location.

There had been dirty water on the floor around the

toilet. The Monstros City Police crime-scene reports of the break-ins all made note of wet bathroom floors, but the police hadn't seen that detail for what it was.

A clue.

At first, Archebold had accused Billy of having an embarrassing accident, but once Billy had explained, the gears in the goblin's head had begun to turn.

And that was when they'd consulted the *Book of Creeps*.

"Sausage?" Archebold asked, pulling Billy from his thoughts.

Billy stared through the lenses of his special Owlboy goggles at the meat product wiggling in his face and felt his stomach do a triple somersault. "No, thank you," he said. Just the thought of eating while enduring the nauseating stench of the sewer was enough to make him ralph, but he managed to keep the contents of his belly where they belonged. "How can you even think of eating down here?"

The goblin tore into his snack with relish. "Obviously you've never been around the old goblins' rest home on franks and beans night," he said, chewing happily. "There's an aroma you could bang nails into. This is nothing."

Billy couldn't imagine anything smelling worse than this place, and he had an awesome imagination.

"Where do you think they are?" he asked impatiently.

Archebold finished his snack and slipped the empty wrapper into the pocket of his tuxedo jacket. "Probably plundering another house."

"They" were the Sludge Sloggers, a jelly-bodied species that could squeeze into the tightest places and, according to the *Book of Creeps*, had been known to slog through the pipes of the Monstros City sewer system. The Sloggers could very easily have traveled those same pipes and used the toilets as their entry and exit points to the burgled homes.

Can we say Ewww, boys and girls?

"So did the other Owlboys ever have trouble with the Sloggers?" Billy asked, wondering how his predecessors had dealt with the foul odor of the sewers.

Archebold seemed to stiffen for a second before slowly turning to look at him. "Y'know, now that you mention it, the Sloggers really aren't the sharpest knives in the drawer. They've never been involved with anything more criminal than stuffing up somebody's pipes and causing their toilet to overflow. Robbery is a whole new game for them." The goblin stroked his chin in thought. "That was a good question, sir, and it certainly has my brain juices flowing."

"Thanks," Billy said. He was just about to suggest

that maybe the robbers were actually the Slime Sliders (a whole other foul, jelly-bodied beastie he'd read about in the *Book of Creeps*) when a rushing roar filled the confines of the smelly stone tunnel.

"Showtime," he heard Archebold say over the thunderous sound.

The tiny goblin began to inch his way toward the source of the racket, and Billy followed close behind.

A powerful wave of raw sewage was pouring into the main tunnel, where it would be filtered and cleaned and eventually flow into the Abominous River. Everything that found its way into the Monstros City sewer system wound up here, and that included Sludge Sloggers.

Torrents of filthy water spewed into the drainage tunnel from a circular opening in the curved wall, and even though Billy couldn't believe it was possible, the smell got worse.

"Ready?" Archebold asked.

"Ready for what?" Billy was eyeing every disgusting fragment of filth that erupted from the drain.

"You've been doing so well, sometimes I forget you're still a rookie," the goblin commented.

Realizing that he must be missing something, Billy squinted through his goggles. And then he saw them. At first they looked like wriggling clumps of clear jelly, plopping down into the filthy water, one after the other, to bob among the other pieces of floating debris.

"Should I be paying attention to them?" Billy asked, pointing at the oily globules wobbling around the out-skirts of the sewage flow.

"Might be a good idea," Archebold answered.

Billy stared hard in concentration. There had to be at least a hundred of the things. He was expecting them all to drift through the drainage pipe with the rest of the sewage when he noticed that they were actually moving against the current, bumping and flowing into each other, making even bigger globs.

"Let me guess," Billy said, watching as the collected blobs began to take more monstrous shapes. "Sludge Sloggers."

"Give the kid in the Owlboy costume a prize," Archebold said.

Soon all the blobs had found their places somewhere on the bodies of eight Sloggers, who stood knee-deep in the raw sewage, giving each other high fives.

Their bodies were the color of hamburger grease, with large potbellies that jiggled as they congratulated each other on a job well done. Something on one of the creatures' rounded stomachs caught Billy's eye. He focused and realized that he could see through the slimy flesh of the monsters' low-hanging bellies, inside which floated bracelets, necklaces, rings and other valuables.

"They carry the stuff they stole in their bellies?" Billy asked, wrinkling his nose.

"You should see how they get it out." Archebold stuck one of his nubby fingers down his throat and pretended to throw up.

Maybe it was the horrible smell of the sewer, or the fact that he hadn't had anything to eat since coming to Monstros City earlier that night, but Billy's stomach suddenly did a quadruple flip, and he made a pretty disgusting gagging sound.

"Good one," Archebold said as the Sludge Sloggers slowly turned to look at them, surprised.

"Sorry. My mother always said I had a strong gag reflex," Billy tried to explain.

"You don't say," Archebold responded with a grumble.

The Sludge Sloggers fixed their black button eyes upon Billy and Archebold, their froglike mouths opening in a gurgling roar. The monsters splashed toward them, their dripping, four-fingered hands reaching out, ready to grab.

"I'll take it from here," Billy said in an effort to make amends. He puffed out his chest and stepped in front of Archebold. "Halt right there, vile creatures!" Billy's voice boomed, echoing about the confines of the stone tunnel as he held up a gloved hand.

And the Sloggers did exactly as they were told, stopping in their tracks.

Billy smiled, lowering his hand.

"Obviously you know a struggle against me would be futile," he said in his best authoritative superhero voice. "So if you would be so kind as to . . . eh . . . ummmm . . ." He wasn't sure what to ask them to do, and looked to Archebold for suggestions.

"You want them to give up the jewelry," the goblin said out of the corner of his mouth. "Ask them to throw up the loot."

Billy turned his attention back to the Sloggers. "Please . . . please throw up the belongings you've stolen so we can return them to their rightful owners."

One of the Sludge Sloggers pointed a dripping finger at him. "Who you?" the creature asked in a wet gurgle.

Billy was stunned. "Why, I'm Owlboy, of course," he proclaimed, sticking out his chest even farther and striking a pose.

The Slogger who had asked the question looked at his brothers, and they started to laugh, sounding like a hundred whoopee cushions all going off at exactly the same time. A disturbing sound, to say the least.

"You no Owlboy," the Sludge Slogger said with a shake of his dripping head.

The others shook their heads in agreement, causing droplets of ooze to fly.

"Owlboy go away long, long time ago."

Billy agreed with Archebold's assessment that the Sloggers were none too bright. Here he was, in his full Owlboy costume, and they still couldn't get it through their jelly-filled heads.

"Well, as you can see as clearly as the noses on your faces, I'm back."

He felt a tug on his cape and turned slightly to see what Archebold wanted.

"Yeah?"

"They don't have noses," the goblin whispered.

"Oh," Billy said, feeling a little embarrassed. "Forget the noses, you can all see that I'm back," he said, spreading his arms to show off his costume. "And better than ever."

The Sloggers stared.

"Who's back?" the one who had been speaking suddenly asked.

Billy slapped his hand to his forehead. These guys were as dumb as a bag of hammers . . . and that was being exceptionally mean to hammers everywhere.

"Owlboy, you dopes," he said in exasperation. "So

make it easy on yourselves and give up the property you stole and we'll see how fast we can get you guys into a nice comfortable jail cell. How's that sound?"

The spokes-Slogger rubbed his bulbous belly, and Billy watched as rings and a wristwatch swirled within.

"We no go to jail," the Slogger stated, slowly shaking his head, and as before, the others shook theirs. "We sell pretty, pretty jewels and stuff to guys who hire us, get lots of money and buy very own sludge pit on outskirts of city. Dat be de life, eh, fellas? No more sewers for us."

The Sludge Sloggers started to give each other high fives again.

"Hate to burst your sludgy bubble," Billy said, pulling on the ends of his gloves for a tighter fit. "But you guys aren't buying anything anytime soon. You're heading to the monster Big House, and I'm the guy who's going to put you there."

The lead Slogger's face twisted into a horrible smile.

"No, you the little guy who gonna try . . ."

Suddenly the Sludge Sloggers were moving incredibly fast, bumping and flowing into one another to form one really big, ticked-off, nasty Slogger. ". . . and fail!" the huge Slogger bellowed.

Billy hadn't seen that one coming.

The slimy beast was at least fifteen feet tall now, and

had to crouch so its head didn't scrape on the rounded ceiling of the sewer. He surged through the filthy water, raising a huge fist, preparing to bring it down on the young superhero and his companion.

"I didn't know they could do that!" Billy yelled, turning to run.

Archebold was quickly flipping through the *Book of Creeps*, searching for additional info. "Me neither. I can't find anything about Sloggers being able to merge to make giant Sloggers. I know a publisher who's going to be getting a nasty letter," the goblin said indignantly.

Billy snatched up the diminutive Archebold from the stone walkway and stuck him under his arm. "I'll help you with that letter if we make it out of here alive," he said, feeling the Slogger's fist strike the ground behind him with enough force to make the rock beneath his feet tremble.

He almost stumbled, but managed to catch himself. Once again he was grateful that being in Monstros City had the strange effect of magnifying his talents big-time. He would never have been able to run this fast back in Bradbury.

But the Slogger was no slouch in the speed department either. Billy remembered reading that the bottoms of Sloggers' feet were ultraslimy, which allowed them to slide across surfaces like an ice-skater crossing a frozen pond.

"Whatcha runnin' for, little Owlboy?" the giant creature gurgled close behind him. "Thought you gonna put me . . . *us* in jail?"

Billy was running as fast as he could, Archebold tucked beneath his arm.

"I can't believe this," the goblin complained. "What good is a book of creeps if it doesn't have all the facts?"

Ahead of them, the tunnel curved, and Billy thought he recognized where they had first come into the stinking sewer system. Sure enough, he saw the black metal ladder that would take them back up to the surface.

He was pouring on the speed, aiming for the ladder, when there was a sudden rush from the water-filled canal to his left. Something large was swimming through the filthy drainage, surging out of the stinking sewage to block his way to freedom.

"You no think it was gonna be that easy, did ya?" the Slogger asked. The monster started to laugh, all the jewelry and valuables stolen by the other Sloggers now swimming around in the disgusting fluids visible through the skin of the giant Slogger's stomach.

Billy backed up, the grumbling Archebold still clutched beneath his arm, flipping angrily through the pages of his book. "Any suggestions?" Billy asked, setting the goblin down.

Archebold continued to turn the pages of the *Book of Creeps*, then suddenly stopped.

"Aha!" he screeched. "Here it is. It was sent as an insert and I must've put it in the wrong place."

The Slogger drew closer, the stink of his gigantic body making Billy swoon. If they didn't get out of the sewer soon, he was going to throw up for sure.

"Yep, additional information made available recently from the Society for the Study of Slimy Beasts of All Varieties states that Sludge Sloggers have the unique ability to join their bodies to create what is known as a King Slogger."

The goblin looked up from the misplaced pages, a smile of victory on his ugly face. "And all is right with the world."

"Not really." Billy pointed to the advancing King Slogger.

"Oh dear," Archebold said with a start. "Don't you think you should be doing something to stop him?"

The King Slogger opened its mouth wider and wider, a disgusting smell like the most rotten pile of garbage in the world wafting out. It was obvious what the great beast intended, and Billy wanted nothing to do with it.

"So how were we going to stop these things?" Billy asked.

Archebold started to go through the book again. "Give me a sec," he said.

"We don't have a sec," Billy responded, the creature's hungry mouth—a tidal wave of filth—starting its disgusting descent to engulf them.

Billy reached into one of the pouches on his utility belt, his fingers fumbling over anything that could possibly be of use. Chewing gum, an extralong rubber band, a plastic container of breath mints, a hunk of lint and the prototype for a freeze bomb.

Stop the presses!

He'd forgotten all about the explosive device he had been working on back at the Roost. When detonated, the bomb would duplicate the raw power of the coldest New England winter, or at least that was his plan. He had been meaning to try the device out when he and Archebold were called away to investigate the burglary, and he had placed the freeze bomb in one of his pouches for safekeeping.

Sometimes he was a genius without even knowing it.

He moved with the speed of an owl, which he imagined had to be pretty fast. Dropping onto his back, he took the extralong elastic, pulled it back as far as he could and shot the freeze-bomb prototype into the yawning mouth of the Sludge Slogger.

"Choke on that!" he shrieked as the bomb rocketed into the monster's cavernous mouth, ricocheting off the roof and down its throat.

The King Slogger reacted immediately, pulling back and placing an oozing hand to his throat.

"What you do?" it asked, its large black eyes bugging out of its head.

"Give it a second and we'll see," Billy said, still lying on his back, looking up at the monster.

And then from within the body of the gelatinous creature there was a silent explosion of blue light. The King Slogger's body went suddenly stiff. A pathetic scream cut off as the slimy and dripping surface of his flesh became solid and all the fluids inside the gigantic beast were turned to ice.

Billy climbed to his feet, wiping the dirt and slime from his costume.

"You want to know what I did?" he asked the frozen monster. "I stopped you cold."

Placing the *Book of Creeps* beneath his arm, Archebold started to clap.

"Very good, sir," the goblin said, applauding. "Very good indeed."

* * *

"Earth to Billy Hooten, come in, Mr. Hooten."

The voice startled Billy from his memories of the previous night's superheroic escapades. He looked up to see his world history teacher, Mr. Cheever, standing in front of his desk with a smile.

"If I remember correctly, we're studying the Roman Empire." The big man placed his hands on his wide hips. "And won't get anywhere near the formation of the space program until at least May, so if you would be so kind as to come down out of orbit and join the class, I would greatly appreciate it."

The rest of the class started to laugh. Billy had no clue as to the current topic of discussion. All he could do was sit with a dopey grin on his face and hope that Mr. Cheever would get tired of teasing him.

Mr. Cheever's eyes twinkled as he prepared to make Billy look like the president of Moronica. "It's the time of year, isn't it, Mr. Hooten?" the teacher asked.

"Time of year, sir?" Billy was beginning to suspect a trap.

Mr. Cheever inhaled loudly, filling his lungs as he looked dreamily about the classroom, his gaze finally resting on the windows. "That smoky smell, the falling leaves, the change in seasons. It's *that* time of year again." He looked back at Billy and his eyes seemed to do a little dance. "The fall. October. Halloween."

A tingle of anticipation shot through Billy's stomach.

He'd been so busy with schoolwork and being Owlboy that he'd almost forgotten Halloween was just around the corner.

"I've always loved this time of year myself," the history teacher said. "I remember when I was your age."

The image of Mr. Cheever marching alongside Roman soldiers filled Billy's head, even though he knew the man wasn't quite that old.

"It was always a huge distraction for me," Mr. Cheever said to the class. "So I can understand how it would be hard for Mr. Hooten here to concentrate."

Mr. Cheever strolled away from Billy's desk.

"I bet you're all excited about the big Halloween costume competition, and how your costume is going to be the best one again this year," the big man said with a smile. "C'mon, Mr. Hooten, share with us. What are you going to be for the contest Saturday night?"

Billy was confused. "You mean next Saturday, don't you?" he asked. The Connery Elementary School Costume Extravaganza was always held the Saturday before Halloween, which, as far as he knew, was at least a week away.

Mr. Cheever stared at the boy, a smirk playing at the corners of his mouth. "No," he said. "I mean this Saturday."

He walked toward a large calendar hanging on the wall and studied the month of October.

"Unless I'm looking at the wrong year," he said, "the last Saturday before Halloween falls this weekend." He turned his head to look at Billy. "Would you like to double-check?"

Billy couldn't help himself. He got up and practically ran to the calendar. Mr. Cheever stepped aside to let him get a good look.

"Holy crap!" Billy exclaimed. His teacher was right.

How could I be so stupid? he thought, reaching out to touch the dates on the calendar. In his mind he still had a week . . . a week to design and make his prizewinning Halloween costume.

But that wasn't the case at all.

Billy only had three days.

CHAPTER 2

How could I be so clueless?

Billy trudged down the stairs to the lunchroom, the weight of his own stupidity on the verge of crushing him flatter than a pancake.

He'd lost a week. How was that even possible? His mind rolled through the last few days—homework, Monstros City, Sludge Sloggers—and he could almost understand how he'd lost track of time. But to forget about the Connery Elementary School Costume Extravaganza? It was unheard of.

He reached the cafeteria and headed for the table where his friends were already eating their lunches.

"Hey, guys, look who it is," Dwight said with a smirk,

making sure everybody was listening. "I'm surprised he remembered he has lunch now."

"You're a riot, Dwight." Billy plopped down in the seat beside Kathy B. "Wish I could forget what a dweeb you are."

That comment got a bigger laugh than Dwight's, and the boy immediately quieted down, shoving Cheez Doodles into his mouth one after another and glowering at everyone. Dwight believed himself to be the coolest and best at everything, even though most of the time he wasn't even close.

"Score one for the Hooten kid," Kathy B said, patting Billy on the back. "How you doing today, Bill? You seem a little out of it."

Billy shrugged, setting his lunch bag down on the table. "Got a lot on my mind," he replied, taking his peanut butter and jelly sandwich out of the bag.

Kathy B suddenly stood and cleared her throat. "Old men forget; yet all shall be forgot," she proclaimed, and then she bowed her head, fist clutched against her chest.

"Let me guess, Shakespeare," Billy said. For as long as he'd known the girl, Kathy B would quote from the writings of William Shakespeare and expect the others to know what she was talking about.

"Yeah, but what play?" she asked as she sat down to finish her lunch.

Billy thought about guessing but decided not to bother. He hoped that someday she would quote from something he knew, like comic books or horror movies. "Don't know," he said, taking a bite of his sandwich.

"It's from *King Henry the Fifth*," she told him, shaking her head. "I would've thought one of you doofuses would get it." She looked at the others at the table with disappointment.

"I thought it might've been from that new show, 'Rapping with the Stars.' I love that show," Reggie Stevens said, grinning through braces that made his mouth look like it was imprisoned in some medieval torture device.

"Good one, Reg," Kathy B said sarcastically.

"Better than his usual 'Green Eggs and Hamlet' answer," Danny Ashwell piped up before biting into his sloppy joe. "Gotta give him points for variety."

Reggie tipped an invisible hat toward his friend.

"Whatever," Kathy B moaned with an overly dramatic roll of her eyes. "So what gives, Billy? You didn't really forget that the costume contest is this week . . . did you?"

The table was suddenly very quiet, all eyes upon him.

Billy wanted to laugh it off, to tell everybody that this was part of an elaborate plan to make them all let

22

their guard down and think his costume would be nothing special and easy to beat this year. He wanted to tell them that in fact he'd been working on the most spectacular costume ever and was ready to win first prize, as he had for the last three years.

But it would've been a lie.

"I honestly thought I had another week," he said sheepishly, looking up from what was left of his PB&J.

Danny Ashwell dropped the spoon he'd been using to shovel fluorescent green Jell-O into his mouth. "Could it be that this year . . . this year the rest of us might actually have a chance at winning this thing?"

Dwight sat back in his chair, smiling. "You won't believe the costume I have this year. Might as well hand over first prize now."

"I think mine might give you a run for your money," Danny said, wiping Jell-O from his face with a napkin. "Guess we'll just have to see, won't we?"

"And wait until you see my costume!" Reggie piped up, so excited he had to stand. "At first I didn't think it was any good, because Billy's is always better, but if his costume stinks, I think I might just win!"

Kathy B grinned from ear to ear. "Do I smell an actual competition this year?" She rubbed her hands together eagerly.

Billy couldn't believe his ears. These were his

friends . . . at least, he thought they were. And they were all plotting against him.

It was an outrage.

"It's not like I haven't been planning, y'know," he said, gathering up his trash and squeezing it into a tight ball.

"So you *do* have a costume then?" Dwight asked.

Everybody at the table leaned forward, eager to hear his answer.

Billy said nothing, squeezing his trash ball tighter.

He felt Kathy B's elbow jam into his ribs. "C'mon, Billy, if you can't tell us, who can ya tell?"

"No," he croaked, the words not wanting to leave his mouth. "I don't have anything yet."

The table went wild with whoops and cheers and high fives all around. And then, as if he weren't even there, they began to chatter about how cool their costumes were and how they all were going to win for sure.

Fine, Billy thought, gathering up his trash. He would find a nice quiet table and begin thinking about his costume. There wasn't any problem. He had plenty of time to put it all together before Saturday night.

No problem at all.

He got up abruptly from his chair and walked straight into the grinning jack-o'-lantern face of Randy

Kulkowski, his mortal enemy and the meanest sixth grader who had ever walked the halls of Connery Elementary.

"Hey there, Hooten," Randy said through a large mouthful of uneven, yellow teeth. His breath stank of raw meat, as if he'd just taken a big bite out of a cow the lunch ladies had stored in back just for him. "Hear there's a bit of a problem with your costume this year."

Mitchell Spivey, Randy's evil little flunky, stood beside his master, rubbing his hands with glee.

"Not really." Billy tried to maneuver around them to throw his trash away, but Randy blocked his path.

"You might as well tell 'em, Billy," a hyper Reggie said, sucking back spit that was attempting to leak from his braces. "He'll only find out the truth anyway after beating one of us up."

"That's true," Randy said with a sadistic grin. "What's going on with your costume?"

Again, Billy wished he could lie. It would have made things so much easier.

"I haven't had a chance to work on it yet," he blurted.

Randy let out an ear-splitting guffaw that Billy was sure could be heard on the second floor of the building. Mitchell laughed as well, bending over as if he'd just heard the funniest joke ever.

"What's so funny?" Billy asked, finally pushing his way around Randy and throwing out his garbage.

The bully crossed his arms. "I just find it funny that *this* would be the year you screwed up."

Billy didn't understand. "Why? What's so special about this year?"

Randy grinned from ear to ear, and Billy thought his head would split in two.

"Cause this is the year that Hero's Hovel coughs up a hundred-dollar gift certificate, and since my costume is going to kick absolute butt, you don't stand a chance no matter how good yours is." He turned his attention back to Billy's so-called friends. "And that goes for you girls as well." Then he turned and lumbered away, cackling.

Billy felt as though his world had suddenly come to an end. *How could I be so stupid?* Hero's Hovel was his all-time favorite comic book store. How could he have forgotten that after all the years of awarding gold ribbons and candy-filled pumpkins, they had decided to spice things up a bit, and Hero's Hovel had volunteered a prize? Behind him, his friends were carrying on, each one trying to be heard over the other.

"I could've won!" "You're crazy, this was my year!" "It's not fair, I tell you!"

Billy wandered, unnoticed, from the lunchroom. He had a lot of thinking to do.

* * *

"I'm getting old," Billy said, helping himself to a second serving of house-fried rice from the Chinese Dragon.

The coffee table was covered in Chinese food take-out boxes, the usual Friday night fare in the Hooten household. Mrs. Hooten sat on the edge of the love seat, plate in hand, while Mr. Hooten lounged in his recliner, his overflowing plate resting on his belly. Billy sat on the floor.

There was no response from either of his parents, so he tried another tactic.

"I sure am frustrated," he said, loud enough to be heard over the DVD rental, an action movie he was sure they had seen at least three times. That was the problem with letting Dad pick the movie; he only liked stuff he'd seen before.

A bus exploded in a ball of fire, and still nobody was listening to him.

"I'm frustrated!" Billy suddenly shouted.

Both his mom and dad were looking at him now, their expressions confused.

"What the heck do you have to be frustrated about?" his dad grumbled, shoveling a forkful of mushu pork into his mouth. "You're only twelve." His gaze wandered back to the TV where the hero had just made an explosive out of a cantaloupe, some Tic Tacs and a cell phone battery.

"What is it, dear?" his mom asked, taking a sip from her glass of water. "What's got you all worked up . . . is it a girl?"

She was suddenly beaming, her eyebrows going up and down. Billy was horrified; that's all he needed.

"What's her name, and what didn't she do that's got you all upset?"

"She didn't do anything," he stammered. "Wait a minute, there is no she!"

"That's fine," his mom said with a sly smile as she helped herself to some more rice. "I don't need to know her name."

Billy shook his head furiously. "That's not what this is about. There is no girl."

His mom nodded, attempting to suppress her smile. "Aha," she said. "No girl problems here, you little devil."

Forgetting that he had a plate of food in his lap, Billy scrambled to stand. "This isn't about that," he said, his voice becoming high-pitched and screechy. "It's way more important than some stupid girl." His mother just stared, a forkful of house fried rice midway to her mouth as Billy continued to rant.

"This could affect me for the rest of my life, destroy my self-esteem, now, in these my most formative years. I may never recover."

Billy stopped, his breath coming in short gasps. His parents were staring at him, and by the looks on their faces, he could see that they were finally with him.

"If not a cute little girl, then what?" his mother asked.

"Yeah," echoed his dad. "What's got your panties in such a bunch?"

Billy took a few deep breaths. "The Halloween Costume Extravaganza is this weekend," he said, pausing for effect. "And I haven't come up with a costume yet."

There was little change in his parents' expressions; the shock of what he'd just told them was obviously too much for them to handle.

"I know, it's how I felt too," Billy continued. "And then I find out that my friends are actually excited that I haven't come up with anything yet." Billy shook his head in disappointment. "I guess you never really know somebody."

His dad was the first to speak. "Is that it?"

Billy didn't understand. "What . . . what do you mean, is that it?"

"Is that what you're all lathered up about?" his dad

asked with a confused tilt of his head. Obviously, he'd failed to grasp the enormity of the situation.

"You're not getting it," Billy tried to explain. "I don't have a costume yet, my friends are all against me, and, to make matters worse, Randy Kulkowski says that his costume is the greatest one ever."

Mr. Hooten helped himself to a chicken finger and waved it around like a magic wand. "Thought this costume business was supposed to be about having fun," he grumbled, turning his attention back to the movie.

Billy couldn't believe it. His father was actually blowing off this cataclysmic situation as if it were nothing important. He stood there, mouth open wide enough to catch flies, not knowing how to respond.

"Don't you worry about a thing, honey," his mother said as she got up from the love seat and started to clean up. "Let me get these leftovers in the fridge and we'll sit down and see what we can come up with."

His vocal cords were practically paralyzed. How could they not understand the enormity of this situation?

"This'll be fun," his mother said as she stacked their dirty plates and headed to the kitchen. "It's been ages since I worked on one of your Halloween costumes."

Images from an old photo album exploded inside Billy's brain—four years old and dressed as a sunflower.

He shivered at the memory. Something that horrific couldn't be allowed to happen again.

"That's okay, Mom," he called after her. "I think I'm going to go up to my room and start working on some designs."

He heard the sound of the dishes being placed in the sink.

"Are you sure?" she asked from the doorway, wiping her hands on a dishtowel. "I've got some really good ideas."

"That's fine, thanks anyway," he told her.

"I've got two words for you, though," she said, coming back for the Chinese food containers that still littered the top of the coffee table. "Monkey ballerina." A crazy grin spread across her face as she slowly nodded. "I'll let you have that one for free, just to show you that your old ma knows what she's doing here."

"Thanks," is all Billy could muster as he slowly backed out of the living room, heading for the stairs that would allow him to escape to his bedroom.

"Just remember," she called after him, "there's plenty more genius where that came from."

❧

Billy closed his bedroom door quickly behind him.

More often than not, his parents didn't understand

the enormity of his predicaments. It reminded him of when he'd been having a heck of a time recently reaching the top level in his Galactic Conqueror game and had found himself on the verge of a nervous breakdown. He'd gotten the same empty stares, and a story from his father about how when he was a kid, they'd had to make do with rocks and dead animals they found in the woods if they wanted something to play with.

Yeah, right.

It was as if adults had something put into their heads after they'd grown up—a computer chip or something—to make it so they couldn't understand their kids.

Billy sighed and went to his bed. He didn't know how to begin. But then his eyes fell on his closet door.

A trip to Monstros might do the trick, he thought. A night of fighting evil always took his mind off things that were troubling him. He sprang from the bed toward the closet, but stopped midway.

But it wouldn't help solve the problem, he realized, and again felt his frustration begin to rise. A trip to Monstros would be a blast, but it wouldn't do a thing to help his costume dilemma.

"All right, get ahold of yourself, Billy," he said sternly.

He knew what he had to do, and that he had to do it

now if he wanted a chance at winning that hundred-dollar gift certificate.

Billy pulled open the bottom drawer of his desk and removed a drawing pad and a pencil. He wasn't going to bed until he came up with the best costume idea ever.

He sat down at the desk, switched on his lamp and waited for the lightning bolt of inspiration to strike. The point of his pencil rested on the white paper, but nothing happened.

He started to get nervous. Prickles of sweat began to break out all over his body, making him feel like there were bugs crawling all over him.

"C'mon, c'mon," he muttered, trying to picture something inside his head that urged him to draw—to create.

But nothing came.

He wished he had a bottle of Zap cola; with all its caffeine and sugar he'd have come up with twenty prizewinning costumes by now. It was like hearing the sound of a dial tone coming from inside his brain—nobody in charge of creativity was home right now.

Billy forced himself to draw a circle so he wouldn't have to stare at the blank piece of paper any longer. The pencil started moving. A subconscious part of his brain had taken over and he allowed it to, wondering what it could be drawing. At first he thought they might be scales, like on some prehistoric reptile, or maybe even sections of body armor, but then he realized exactly what they were.

Flower petals.

He was drawing a big sunflower.

"*Yeeek!*" Billy cried, tearing the page from the notebook and tossing it across the room. That would be the last time he trusted his subconscious.

He got up from his chair. "I need inspiration," he said aloud, going toward his closet again. He pulled open the door, not looking to the back where his Owlboy costume hung—he didn't want to be tempted—and hauled out a box.

If anything was going to inspire him, it would be this. He removed the cover to the box and exposed the old comics inside. The smell of old paper wafted up and Billy closed his eyes, taking a deep breath. There was nothing like that old comic book smell.

He reached inside and pulled out the first stack. These were his prized possessions, his very own Owlboy comics. He had saved up his allowance and then won a few bids on BuyBay—with his parents' permission, of course—after he'd had to return the ones that Cole, the owner of Hero's Hovel, had lent him.

If anything was going to inspire him to greatness,

it would be these. He sat down on the floor with his back against his bed and started flipping through the colorful pages.

He had gone through more than half the box when he felt his eyes start to get heavy. He promised himself he would only close them for a minute, but as soon as they were shut, he felt himself being sucked into the darkness, deeper and deeper, until he was fast asleep.

Billy was sitting on the floor of Michelangelo's Sandwich Shop and Pizzeria. It was one of his favorite places to have lunch when he and his parents were out.

"What're you going to have, sport?" asked a powerful voice from up front at the store's counter.

Billy got to his feet, staring in awe at the muscular back of a costumed hero. He knew immediately who it was. Owlboy—not Billy, but Owlboy from the pages of the old comics—turned around to look at him.

"C'mon, Bill," he said with a dazzling, white smile. "Let's not keep the nice gentleman waiting."

A gorilla wearing a white paper hat and an apron stood behind the counter.

"Um . . . I'll have a chicken finger sandwich, lettuce, tomato and a little mayo."

The gorilla let out a roar that would've made Kong

proud and went to work making the sandwich. After what seemed like only seconds, the great ape placed a tray with two sandwiches and two drinks on top of the counter.

"Thank you, my good man," Owlboy said, paying the gorilla with five bananas before taking the tray in his gloved hands.

Five bananas, Billy thought. *Prices certainly have gone up.*

"Should we find a place to sit?" the costumed hero asked.

"Sure," Billy answered, looking around the restaurant. There wasn't anybody else in the place. "How about over there?" Billy suggested, pointing to an orange booth in the corner.

"Excellent eye," the hero said, heading in that direction.

The two sat down, the original Owlboy taking Billy's sandwich from the tray and placing it down in front of him.

"The food of the gods, my friend. Eat up." Owlboy unwrapped his own sandwich. His eyes danced behind his goggles and he licked his lips. "Haven't had one of Michelangelo's steak bombs in a dog's age," he said as he took half of the mighty sandwich in his hand.

This is incredibly bizarre, Billy thought. He took a sip of his drink and was surprised to taste the sugary goodness of Zap cola.

Owlboy took a bite of his overstuffed sandwich, meat and vegetables spilling onto the wax paper wrapping.

"What a mess," he said through a mouthful of food, reaching for a napkin from the container on the table and wiping his mouth. Some grease had gotten on his goggles and he wiped them. "But it wouldn't be a Michelangelo's steak bomb without it." The superhero laughed heartily.

Billy nodded, smiling at the comic book hero. He couldn't hold it back any longer.

"What are we doing here?" he asked.

Owlboy had helped himself to some more napkins. "Thought it was obvious, sport," the superhero said. "We're having some lunch, and we're about to discuss a little problem I hear you've been having in the creativity department." The hero winked at him from behind the tinted glass of his goggles.

"My contest costume?" Billy asked, eyes wide and eager. "Can you help me?"

Owlboy chuckled before taking another huge bite of his sandwich.

"Of course I can," he said, reaching across the table

to give Billy a gentle punch in the arm. "Us super-types have to stick together."

Suddenly hungry, Billy dug into his own sandwich. If anybody could come up with something that would blow the socks off the Connery Elementary School costume contest judges, it was a comic book superhero.

They continued to eat in silence. Billy's anticipation was growing, but he didn't want to rush his hero. Owlboy continued to eat and eat. And just when Billy thought he might be finished, there seemed to be yet more food on his tray.

If there was one thing Billy learned while sitting there waiting for the comic book adventurer, it was that he was a real slob. Pieces of meat and cheese dangled from the corners of his mouth, to be joined by smears of ketchup as he finished an extra-large order of French fries.

Finally, Billy couldn't wait anymore. "Do you think we could talk about my Halloween costume now?" he asked, hoping that he wasn't being rude.

Owlboy searched his tray for stray fries. "Of course," he said, popping some extra-crispy stragglers in his mouth. "I'm pretty much finished here."

Eagerly, Billy picked up the tray of trash and disposed of it in the closest barrel.

"So what are you thinking?" he asked, returning to the booth.

The hero stroked his prominent chin. "I'm thinking of something that's never been attempted before," he said, eyes dancing behind his goggles.

"Something really scary?" Billy asked, his voice a whisper.

The hero shook his head. "No, everybody's done scary, I'm thinking exciting . . . thrilling. Something that will fill the judges with awe."

Billy could barely sit still, he was so excited. "I'm ready," he said.

Owlboy was silent, staring off into space. Billy could practically hear the gears whirring inside the costumed adventurer's head, practically smell the burning plastic as he exercised the superior power of his brain.

"Well?" Billy asked.

The hero lifted his hands from the table. "I'm getting something," he said. "It's coming to me . . . an idea so ahead of its time that you'll be looked upon as a pioneer of Halloween costumes worldwide."

"What is it?" Billy asked, his legs kicking feverishly beneath the table. "Tell me, I'm dyin' here!"

Owlboy reached for a napkin from the holder at the end of the table. "I must show you," he said, placing the napkin down in front of him. He dug into one of the pouches attached to his utility belt and removed a black marker.

The costumed crusader immediately went to work, sketching something out on the napkin. Billy craned his neck, but the way Owlboy had positioned his arm, he couldn't quite see the drawing.

Billy wanted to scream. He was already thinking of ways to use his hundred-dollar gift certificate.

"I'm done," Owlboy finally announced, picking up the napkin so only he could see what he'd drawn. "And if I must say, this is genius personified."

"Let me see," Billy said, starting to giggle uncontrollably. He wasn't sure if he'd ever been so excited, although there was that time with Santa at Pringle's department store when he was four. *That* had resulted in an accident of drenching proportions. Luckily, at this stage in his life, that wasn't really an issue anymore.

"Are you ready to gaze upon the design for this year's winning costume, and perhaps even future years of the Connery Elementary School Costume Extravaganza?"

Billy's mouth moved, but his excitement was so great that no sound came out.

Owlboy turned the napkin around, and Billy looked at it in wonder.

Or was it complete confusion?

"What is it?" he asked, staring at the image of a furry, apelike creature wearing a short dress.

"Don't you see, champ?"

"No . . . I really don't," Billy said, still looking at the crude drawing.

"It's a monkey ballerina," the hero said proudly.

And Billy started to scream.

CHAPTER 3

Monkey ballerina.

Billy shivered, even though he wasn't cold. The memory of his bizarre dream was more disturbing than the last five horror movies he'd seen. Standing on his porch steps, he moved his backpack from one shoulder to the other.

It was a beautiful, crisp Saturday morning, and he'd decided that he needed a trip to Monstros City to clear his head and inspire him with a costume idea.

Billy glanced at his watch. It was still ridiculously early, and his parents wouldn't be up for hours. Just to make sure he had everything, he removed the backpack from his shoulder and opened it. His Owlboy costume and all its accessories were neatly folded inside the bag.

Satisfied, he quietly made his way to the stone wall separating his backyard from the Pine Hill Cemetery.

With little difficulty that had come from lots of practice, Billy hopped up onto the wall and prepared to jump down into the graveyard.

"Hey, you!" called a squeaky voice. Billy turned to see that he was being watched by a little girl, no more than five years old, sitting on a bright-pink Big Wheel and holding a stuffed rabbit in her lap.

The twerp's name was Victoria, and she was his next-door neighbor. She was like a ninja. He hardly ever heard her sneaking up on him.

Billy rolled his eyes, preparing for the inevitable.

"Hey, Victoria," he said, getting ready to ignore her and continue on his way.

"Mr. Flops wants to know what you're doing," she said, holding up the gray stuffed bunny in both hands.

"Just some stuff I gotta take care of," he explained. "Have a nice day."

"What do you gotta do in the cemetery?" she asked in her squeaky little-kid voice.

Billy scowled. "Does Mr. Flops need to know that, too?"

She shook her head, pigtails flopping like crazy antennas. "Nope, I do."

He couldn't believe she'd caught him again. She did

this to him constantly, and every time it happened he promised himself that next time he would just ignore her and continue walking.

Maybe she has some kind of mutant power? It would explain a lot.

"No, you don't," Billy told her. "It's grown-up stuff and I gotta get going before I'm late."

"Want to play with me?" she asked before he could jump down off the wall. She got off her bike and went to the wagon that was attached behind it. "I've got lots of toys you can play with," she coaxed, holding up an action figure and a pom-pom.

Billy shook his head. "Nope, got places to go, things to do."

And as he turned he saw it from out of the corner of his eye, the dreaded quiver in the lip, the big brown eyes filling with tears.

She was going to cry.

He hated that.

"What's wrong now?" he asked with an exasperated sigh.

"I want you to play with me," Victoria answered, her face twisting up as two big fat tears rolled down her plump, red cheeks.

"I can't play with you," he tried to explain. "I gotta do stuff."

Victoria tossed her head back and wailed. It was bad, real bad, and loud too. If she kept this up, she'd wake up the whole neighborhood.

He didn't want to say it. He bit the inside of his mouth to prevent the words from coming, but she'd left him no choice.

"We'll play later," he said over the sound of her tantrum.

Victoria immediately turned off the waterworks.

"When you get back from doing stuff?" she asked with a sniffle.

"Yeah," he said with a sigh, shaking his head. "When I get back from doing stuff."

"Okeydoke. See ya later, alligator," she said cheerfully, and got back on her Big Wheel with Mr. Flops. She did a U-turn in the middle of the yard, pedaling like mad across the grass and down the driveway.

She had done it to him again.

Mutant power, for sure.

Billy walked into the Sprylock family mausoleum like he owned the place. Since discovering the secret world of monsters beneath the Pine Hill Cemetery, and assuming the mantle of Monstros City's astounding superhero, coming and going from the ancient family burial place had become almost second nature.

Standing in the center of the dusty stone structure, Billy removed the backpack from his shoulder and began to put on his Owlboy costume.

He hoped this visit to the city of monsters would fix his mental block about his Halloween costume. Maybe a little crime-fighting would get the creative juices flowing again. The memory of the previous night's dream flashed inside his brain and Billy shuddered.

Monkey ballerina! Never, he thought, slipping on his leather gloves after stepping into his rubber boots. *There has to be something better than that.*

And he hoped that that special something would come to him after some Monstros City superheroics.

Billy slipped the goggles down over his glasses and walked to the back of the burial chamber toward the great stone coffin, as he had done many times in the last few weeks. A strange sensation squirmed around in his belly as he reached the coffin and pushed aside the lid to expose the seemingly bottomless darkness within. It was a feeling he hoped would never go away.

Outside the mausoleum he was just Billy Hooten. But here, he was so much more.

He stepped carefully inside the coffin, wading into the pool of darkness. His boots found the stone steps that would take him into another world, and he started to descend.

Dressed like this, Billy Hooten was Owlboy. A real live superhero.

How cool was that?

CHAPTER 4

Welcome to Monstros City.

The metropolis of monsters hummed like a giant beehive.

Beasties of every conceivable shape, size and color lived and thrived in this secret place—this pocket world located deep beneath the Pine Hill Cemetery in Bradbury, Massachusetts.

It was nighttime in the thriving megalopolis, but then, when wasn't it? It was always night in Monstros, and the creatures that made up its thriving population went about their business; some heading to work, others finishing up their shifts, most just going about their lives, eventually returning to their homes and

monstrous families. The streets were jammed with comings and goings.

The city was alive.

There was a lot of good in Monstros City, but where there was good, there was also the not so good. The return of Owlboy had cut back on criminal activity, but it had not stopped it completely. Evil still existed in the city, hiding in the deepest pools of shadow, waiting for an opportunity to strike.

Waiting for an opportunity very much like this.

The Squids entered the Monstros City savings and loan just about lunchtime.

The bank was bustling with citizens eager to take advantage of the special offer for folks opening a new account.

What monster didn't need a Dr. Mellman's Home Surgery Kit?

But the Squids had come for something else.

"Ladies and gentlemen," the leader, who went by the name of Armstrong, said through a small, box-shaped speaker that he wore around his neck like a fine piece of jewelry. "This is a robbery."

"What did you say?" asked a short, furry monster clutching his brand-new home surgery kit.

Armstrong sighed, one of his slimy tentacles reaching

to turn up the volume on his electronic voice box. The other five squids in his gang, positioned around the bank, adjusted theirs as well.

Squids were notoriously soft-spoken, and used specially designed microphones to enhance their voices.

"I said, this is a robbery!" Armstrong proclaimed, his voice now easier to hear through the crackling speaker. Each of his muscular tentacles held guns that he waved about menacingly. "Does everybody hear me now?"

The other squids produced their weapons as well, showing they meant business. The bank erupted into chaos, the screams and cries of the frightened filling the air.

Armstrong raised a tentacle and fired a shotgun blast into the air. It sounded like thunder, instantly silencing the panicked bank customers.

"That's better," the squid gurgled through his speaker, his bulbous eyes studying them all. "Now give us everything you've got," the leader of the tentacled terrors proclaimed, producing large sacks from within the folds of his many arms. "And don't be stingy with those awesome Dr. Mellman Home Surgery Kits."

"I think congratulations are in order," Sigmund Sassafras said to his sister as he listened through a set of headphones covering large ears which protruded from an even larger head.

Sireena Sassafras reached up and adjusted the rearview mirror in the van, checking to see if she'd evenly applied the bright-red lipstick to her large, swollen lips. Without missing a beat, she raised her palm so that her brother could give her a high five, which is exactly what he did.

"How are they doing?" she asked, smacking her lips and checking her reflection from every angle.

Sigmund smiled. He was glad he'd decided to wire up the squids and experience the thrill of the robbery without the risk. "Excellent. Squids were definitely the way to go."

Sireena looked away from her reflection. "But isn't that what you said about the Sludge Sloggers?"

Sigmund's round eyes bulged. "Don't start that again," he warned, ripping the headphones from his large cranium. "You thought the Sloggers were a good idea too, and just because they encountered some minor difficulties before they could deliver our goods doesn't mean that—"

"Minor difficulties?" Sireena interrupted, bending the mirror back to its original position. "You call being stopped by Owlboy a minor difficulty?"

Sigmund's blood started to boil, and he felt his good

mood begin to disintegrate. "I told you never to mention his name," he growled.

"Whose name?" his sister asked in mock confusion. "Owlboy's name?"

Unable to contain his fury, Sigmund reached out and ran his hand across his sister's moist lips, smudging the freshly applied lipstick all over the side of her face.

Sireena shrieked, grabbing the rearview mirror again to assess the damage.

"Look at what you've done!" she bellowed, attempting to wipe the red smear from her greenish skin.

"I warned you," Sigmund said, shaking a finger at her. "That name is a blight upon the Sassafras family. Have you forgotten what that . . . that . . . *person* did to our parents?"

"Of course I haven't forgotten!" Sireena cried. "Do you seriously believe I could forget that it was Owlboy who thwarted our mother and father's plans to become king and queen of crime in Monstros City? And that we were deprived of their love and affection during our most formative teenage years when Father was banished to Dimension X and Mother was sentenced to serve—is currently serving—sixteen life sentences for crimes against inhumanity in Beelzebub Prison?"

Sigmund felt a slight twinge of guilt. "I'm sorry for

smearing your lipstick," the male half of the Sassafras Siblings muttered, lowering his gaze. "It's just that since Owlboy's . . . I mean, since *that person's* return, my fuse has been running a little short, and sometimes my temper gets away from me."

"That's all right, dear brother," Sireena said, reaching down to the floor to retrieve her Gigantisaurus skin handbag. "And I'm sorry for shooting fifty thousand volts of electricity through your body."

Sigmund paused. "What was that about fifty thousand volts of electricity?" he asked, his face twisted up in confusion.

From inside her handbag Sireena produced her electroshock pistol and fired a crackling bolt of electricity into her brother's chest. She watched him twitch in the driver's seat, a plume of smoke billowing up from the top of his square head. Satisfied, she placed the pistol back in her bottomless purse and returned to fixing her makeup.

Sigmund was about to launch himself across the front seat at her when a faint sound from his discarded headset distracted him. "Did you hear that?" he asked, patting out the flames that burned at the top of his head.

"Hear what?" Sireena asked.

Sigmund picked up the headphones and placed

them over his ears again. "I could've sworn I heard one of the squids say something about . . . an owl."

"What did you say?" Armstrong's voice gurgled from the speaker around his neck. He turned his conical head away from the strange image now shining upon the bank vault door.

"I said, it sort of looks like an owl," the squid (whose name was Tibert) said, studying the strange shadowy image. The bank patrons, who had all been herded together with their paws, feelers and odd appendages behind their heads, agreed.

"But why would there be a shape of an owl on the bank vault door?" the squid boss asked aloud.

Their sacks stuffed with cash and Home Surgery Kits, the other squids approached for a better look.

"Maybe it's just a decoration . . . for Owl Day, perhaps," suggested one.

Another set his overly stuffed bag down on the floor and crossed four of his arms. "This is vaguely familiar to me," the squid's voice crackled through his speaker box.

"Didn't it have something to do with the superhero?" asked another. "You know, the one who disappeared."

"Yeah," the last squid agreed with a nod of his

pointed head. "What was his name again? I think it had something to do with a bird." He snapped his tentacle in the air like a whip, trying to remember.

"Owlboy?" somebody within the savings and loan suggested.

The squids all stopped, considering the answer.

"Who said that?" Armstrong wanted to know. He didn't recognize the voice, and it hadn't come over a speaker, so he knew it wasn't one of his boys.

"I think it came from over there," Tibert said, pointing to the crowd of bank customers.

"I said it," said the mysterious voice again, and one by one the customers of the savings and loan slowly turned their heads to see a small figure dressed in a brown costume and feathered cape jump up onto one of the counters.

"And who are you?" Armstrong asked.

"Thought you woulda figured it out by now," the costumed character said, pointing to the dark image shining on the bank vault door.

"I would've thought it was obvious.

"I'm Owlboy."

CHAPTER 5

And Billy had thought the Sludge Sloggers were dumb.

"Owlboy," said the squid who seemed to be the leader of this gang of dopes. He scratched his chin—at least Billy thought it was a chin—*do squids even have chins?*—with the tip of a tentacle that wasn't holding a gun. "Then that explains the owl symbol on the safe door."

All the squids started to nod as if the secrets of the universe had been revealed to them.

Billy put a gloved hand to his head and shook it in dismay. "Can't fool you, can we?"

Meanwhile, Archebold had emerged from his hiding place at the back of the bank, still holding the portable Owlboy signal. "Can I turn this off?" he hollered.

"Yeah," Billy answered. "No sense in wasting it. We could've had 'Owlboy is in the house' posters, and I still don't think they would've gotten it."

"They're not very bright," Archebold yelled across the room.

"Tell me about it," Billy called back.

The squids were looking at Archebold.

"Who's that?" the leader asked.

"My sidekick," Billy replied.

The squids nodded but remained silent, until at last the leader spoke again.

"So, you're Owlboy, a superhero, and I bet you've come to try to stop us."

Billy folded his arms across his chest. "That's about it, yeah."

That was when things got really crazy. The squids were dumb, there was no doubt about that, but they were also violent.

"Think again," the leader bellowed, his voice so loud it caused his speaker to crackle. "Boys, stuff this bird fulla lead!"

Billy barely had time to react before the entire squid gang aimed their multiple weapons and started to fire at him. *Better me than the customers*, he thought, jumping behind the counter as bullets flew above his head and struck the wall behind him.

He had to put a stop to this before anybody got hurt. Sitting on the floor, he opened all the pouches on his utility belt, but didn't see anything he could use to take down a gang of squids.

He was going to have to improvise.

He started to stand, and roughly banged his head.

"Ouch!" he squeaked. One of the bank tellers had left their drawer open, most likely when they were handing over the cash to the squids. Billy noticed that a section of the drawer was filled with rolls of change.

"Hmm, these might just work," he said, hefting the heavy roll of coins in his hand.

He could hear the squids whispering to one another as they stalked closer to the counter.

"Do you think we got 'im?" one asked.

"I hear him movin' around back there. Maybe we winged him."

Another squid started to giggle. "Winged him, I get it."

"Get what?"

"The joke . . . he's Owlboy . . . a bird . . . and we might've winged him. Pretty funny."

"I don't get it," the squid said.

Billy couldn't stand to listen to these idiots anymore.

Tensing his legs, he sprang from his hiding place, arms filled with rolled coins. "Deposit or withdrawal?" he asked.

The squids gasped, jumping back, multiple limbs attempting to aim multiple weapons.

"How about a deposit?" Billy offered. "Me first." And he began to throw the rolled coins with amazing precision. Even he was impressed by his own accuracy.

It was a blast being a superhero in Monstros City.

The rolled quarters struck the squids exactly between their funky, protruding eyes. One after the other Billy hit the bull's-eye, resisting the urge to laugh as each of the multilimbed criminals went down in a flopping heap.

"Owlboy!" Archebold's squeaky voice called out. Billy glanced up to see the goblin scampering across the bank, *Book of Creeps* in hand. "You might want to be careful because . . ."

But before he could finish, the weirdest thing happened.

An inky explosion erupted from each of the squids, filling the air with a rolling black cloud that made it nearly impossible to see.

Billy jumped down from the counter, searching for his goblin pal. "What the heck is this?" he asked, fumbling through the inky fog.

"I was trying to warn you," came Archebold's voice from somewhere in the artificial darkness. "According to the *Book of Creeps*, when a squid feels threatened, it releases a chemical cloud to aid in its escape. In other words, we've been smoked, sir."

Billy couldn't see anything through the black fog, but then he got an idea. He reached up, fiddling with the button on his special night-vision goggles. Suddenly he saw the shapes of his foes through the rolling smoke. "Bingo!" he cried, watching the squids as they made their way toward the door, and freedom.

Billy started after them, but tripped, falling to the floor.

"Stupid bags," he growled, kicking at the sacks that littered the ground where the squids had abandoned them, causing the money and other contents to spill out onto the floor.

"Are you all right, sir?" Archebold asked, now at his side.

"I'm good," Billy said, kneeling down to take a look at a case that had spilled from one of the loot bags. "Dr. Mellman's Home Surgery Kit? You gotta be kidding me."

Archebold shook his large head. "Oh no, Dr. Mellman is very respected here."

Billy felt a shiver run up and down his spine. His

mother had a Dr. Mellman book that she had gotten at a yard sale before he was born.

Weird.

He opened the lid of the kit and pulled out what looked like a spray can. "What's this?" he asked his companion.

"That's canned anesthesia," the goblin explained. "Careful with that, don't want to knock yourself out."

Billy smiled, an idea blossoming inside his head. He quickly scanned the black fog, seeing that the squids had just about made it to the door.

"Excuse me a minute," he said, taking the canned anesthesia with him. "I've got some squids to apprehend."

With a mighty leap, Billy propelled himself through the squids' escape cloud, landing in front of them just before they exited through the door.

"Going somewhere, ladies?" Billy said.

And before they could raise their weapons, he lifted the can of Dr. Mellman's Home Surgery Kit anesthesia and sprayed it into their squiddy faces—holding his breath, of course, so as not to render himself unconscious.

One by one the squids went down, their limbs like limp spaghetti as they dropped to the floor of the savings and loan, knocked out cold by the canned gas.

The black fog gradually started to clear, and Billy

saw Archebold marching toward him, a gigantic smile plastered on his ugly face.

The bank customers were right behind him.

"Good thinking, sir," the goblin said just as the savings and loan customers began to clap.

And to cheer Billy's name.

"Owlboy! Owlboy! Owlboy!"

Sitting in the van, not too far away from the Monstros City savings and loan, Sireena Sassafras watched her brother turn the most interesting shade of blood red, which was quite a trick, seeing as his skin was usually green.

"What's the matter now?" she asked, sliding away from him. It wasn't good when he got like this. This she knew for a fact, because she often reacted in the exact same way.

"It's him!" Sigmund screamed. "He's done it to us again!"

"Who?" she demanded, certain that she already knew the answer but wanting to be absolutely sure. "Who? Who?"

"Exactly," her brother growled, removing the headphones from his large head and shoving them in her face so she could hear.

"*Owlboy! Owlboy! Owlboy! Owlboy!*"

Sireena felt her own face begin to contort in rage.

"Owlboy," she spat, flexing her fingers, the freshly polished bright-red claws eager to rip something apart. "What should we do?" she asked, hoping her brother had some sort of answer, though she doubted it.

He wasn't the sharpest knife in the drawer.

Sireena watched as her brother twitched and contorted, the rage that he was attempting to contain threatening to explode from his body.

"I can't take it anymore," he said pathetically, shaking his head from side to side. "Why is he back now? All those years he was nowhere to be found, but as soon as we decide to take our rightful place as the crime bosses of Monstros City, he's back in our faces. It's not fair, I tell you . . . not fair!"

"Get ahold of yourself, Brother," Sireena warned. "Losing your nut isn't going to help anything."

The wailing sounds of police sirens suddenly filled the air.

"The cops!" she screamed, panic setting in.

Sigmund grinned. "Losing your nut isn't going to help anything," he snarled.

She'd had just about enough of him, and jumped across the seat to punch his fat face in.

But Sigmund was ready for her. He wrapped his

hands around her flabby throat, preventing her from getting the upper hand.

Sigmund had been hatched a mere three seconds after Sireena had emerged from her own egg, but from the moment she'd laid eyes on him, she had wished she was an only child. No matter how hard she'd tried over the years to make it a reality, she just couldn't seem to get the job done.

She was hoping today would be her lucky day.

They had fallen into an all too familiar rhythm of biting, punching and kicking, when Sireena heard it over the wails of the approaching police cars: the sound of a powerful engine, rumbling like the hungry stomach of some great beast.

"Do you hear that?" she asked through her brother's filthy fingers as he attempted to pull the flesh on her face over her skull like a hood.

"I hear nothing except the sound of my rage-filled blood pounding in my ears and . . ." Sigmund paused. "What *is* that?" he asked, taking his fingers from his sister's mouth to cup one of his prominent ears.

Sireena climbed off her brother to peer through the driver's-side window at the street outside. From an alley that ran alongside the savings and loan, a strangely shaped yellow car emerged, its engine roaring powerfully.

She was mesmerized by the sight of it.

"That's his car, isn't it?" Sigmund asked, squishing his bulk against the car door so that he too could see.

"Yes, it is," she said, almost in a trance. The vehicle was shaped like the head of a bird—an owl, its slick, metal surface painted a bright, nearly blinding yellow.

The car turned left from the alley, rumbling quickly past them on its way to parts unknown.

Perhaps to some secret location, Sireena thought.

And then another thought wiggled into her mind, like a deadly brain serpent crawling from the ear of its unwary victim.

Sigmund gasped as he saw the multiple police cars pulling up in front of the savings and loan, the law officers scrambling from their vehicles and running into the bank.

"What should we do?" he asked in a frightened whisper.

Sireena pushed her brother out of the way and maneuvered herself behind the steering wheel of the van. The keys were still in the ignition and she started the vehicle, screeching out from their parking space and away from the scene of the crime.

"What are you doing?" Sigmund yelped, fumbling to put his seat belt on.

"We're going hunting, dear brother," she snarled, her eyes focused dead ahead, searching for the yellow vehicle.

"Hunting?" Sigmund asked, not yet getting the picture. "I don't understa—"

"Owl, Sigmund," she cut him off. "We're hunting owl."

The Owlmobile drove through the dark city streets of Monstros City, from Banshee Boulevard onto Vampire Drive, then turning left onto Corpse Crossing.

"Why the long face?" Archebold asked from behind the steering wheel.

Billy looked out the window as the city passed by. Everyone who saw the car—who saw him—started to cheer and wave their claws, or tentacles, or whatever they had. He didn't answer his friend's question.

"Things are going great," Archebold said happily as he drove. "The city is nuts about you, never mind the fact that you just took out an entire gang of armed criminals—well, of course they were armed, they were squids—but that's beside the point," the goblin muttered beneath his breath. "You stopped them from robbing the bank and saved the day. How cool is that?"

Billy forced a smile. "Pretty cool, I'd say."

But the goblin wasn't buying what Billy was trying to sell.

"I'm not the sharpest claw on the paw, but I can tell when something's wrong," Archebold said. "What is it?"

"It's stupid." Billy didn't really want to talk about it, but it was eating him up inside.

"I'll be the judge of that," Archebold reassured him. "Let's hear it."

As Billy prepared to explain, he realized how silly it all was. Here he was in the coolest car that ever existed, driving through the streets of Monstros City after rescuing the savings and loan from a gang of gun-wielding squids, and all he could think about was how he didn't know what he was going to be for the Connery Elementary School Costume Extravaganza.

How lame is that?

Billy turned in his seat toward the goblin and took a deep breath. "Halloween is this week, but I thought it was next week because I've been all confused with schoolwork and being Owlboy and stuff and didn't know what the date was."

The words just spilled from his mouth. He tried to slow them down, but it was like trying to keep Danny Ashwell away from the chocolate pudding at lunch.

He didn't stand a chance.

"But the costume extravaganza is on Saturday night,

and I was like, Saturday night? I haven't even come up with a costume yet and all the guys were like, cool, think we might have a chance of winning this year, and I was like, man, I thought these guys were my friends."

Archebold looked briefly away from the road to stare at him with eyes even wider than usual. "Is that it?" the goblin asked.

"Sort of," Billy said. "Randy Kulkowski says that he's got a Halloween costume so scary and awesome that nobody has a chance of winning, so I need to come up with a really cool idea so he doesn't win the hundred-dollar gift certificate. But no matter how hard I try, I can't seem to come up with anything good, and I think I'm gonna lose."

The goblin was silent as he drove the bright yellow Owlmobile into the Wailing Wood. The headlights illuminated the winding road as the car made its way through the frightening forest.

"Pretty crazy, huh?" Billy said. "I was thinking that maybe you could help me out with some ideas."

Archebold remained quiet, driving the Owlmobile toward the base of a ginormous tree growing up from the center of the Wailing Wood. They headed into a secret passage hidden within the tangle of gargantuan roots that would take them up into Owlboy's headquarters, the Roost.

"Archebold," Billy said, worried that the goblin might think he was crazy, "are . . . are you all right?"

The tiny creature nodded as he pulled the Owl-mobile into the elevator that would bring the car up to the garage.

"Yeah, I'm fine," he said, putting the car in park. "But could you explain what a *hollowbean* is?"

CHAPTER 6

"**A**re you sure he went in there?" Sigmund asked, squinting his beady eyes and staring through the van's windshield at the entrance to the Wailing Wood.

"I'm positive," Sireena replied, squeezing the steering wheel so tightly that she thought it might break apart in her hands. "It's appropriate, don't you think? An owl, living in the woods and all."

"I guess," Sigmund answered. "I've heard rumors that he had a secret hideaway hereabouts."

The inside of the van grew almost deafening with silence, and Sireena couldn't stand it anymore. She threw open the door and climbed out of the vehicle.

"Where are you going?" Sigmund's eyes were wide with fear.

"I'm going into the woods," she said, slamming the door closed and going around to the back of the van.

Sigmund joined her, looking about nervously. "Do you know what they say about this place?" he asked her, his eyes darting in all directions.

"Yes," she said, opening the vehicle's back doors. "That it's the scariest place in Monstros City."

Something rustled in the underbrush and Sigmund practically jumped into her arms. "Did you hear that?" he asked in a frightened gasp.

Sireena flipped a piece of dirty rug from the back of the van floor to reveal a hidden storage compartment underneath. She reached inside the compartment, removing a rifle from its hiding place with other equally dangerous-looking weaponry.

"I heard it," she growled, firing a single shot at the area where the creepy noise had come from. The gun boomed and the trees and bushes around them exploded into fire and smoke. "And I doubt we'll hear it again," she said, resting the still smoldering rifle on her shoulder.

"But what if there's more of . . . of whatever that was?"

"And you call yourself a Sassafras," Sireena scoffed. "Our ogre ancestors would be ashamed."

The Sassafrasses were one of the oldest and nastiest

of the evil ogre families. Their cruelty and really bad moods were legendary in the darker regions of Monstros City, and had been for centuries.

"What are you trying to say?" Sigmund glowered, pushing his ugly face mere inches from hers.

"What I'm trying to say is, if we plan on becoming the true masters of crime in this city, like we promised our parents we would, we need to be proactive."

She reached inside the van for another weapon and handed it to her brother. Sigmund took it from her, tentatively at first, then pulled it roughly from her hands.

"Give me that," he mumbled, checking to see if the gun was loaded before slinging it over his shoulder and starting to walk down the path that would take them deeper into the Wailing Wood. "Well, what are we waiting for?" he asked.

Sireena jogged to catch up, grabbing him by the shoulder.

"I need to know if you're serious about this," she said, pulling her sibling around to face her.

"Of course I am."

"Are you serious enough to swear the Sassafras Siblings oath?" she wanted to know.

Sigmund hesitated momentarily, then decided he was serious enough and prepared to take the oath.

They both spit into their left hands, reached around their heads, twisting their bodies in the weirdest of angles, and proceeded to balance on one foot.

"Do you, Sigmund Sassafras, swear to hunt and destroy, in any way, shape or form possible, Owlboy, superhero and perpetual thorn in the side of the Sassafras family?" Sireena asked her brother.

"Do you, Sireena Sassafras, swear the same, to hunt and destroy, in any way, shape or form, Owlboy, superhero and perpetual thorn in the side of the Sassafras family?"

Their spit-covered hands clasped together as one, sealing the Sassafras Siblings special oath. "I swear," they said in unison, trying not to tumble to the ground as they balanced precariously on one foot each.

Sigmund let go of Sireena's hand first. "Serious enough for you?" he asked, regaining his balance and taking his fearsome weapon from his shoulder.

Sireena retrieved her own rifle. "Let's make our parents proud," she said.

And the two of them walked side by side into the Wailing Wood, searching for the object of their oath.

Searching for their prey.

"Look, for the twelfth time," Billy scolded, "it's Halloween, not hollow beans."

Archebold turned to Halifax, who stood beside him. "I still don't get it, do you?"

Halifax, the troll mechanic who kept all the gadgets and machines inside the Roost running smoothly, shook his shaggy head. "He lost me with the part about the candy."

Billy and Archebold were sitting at a circular table in the Snack Room—just one of the hundreds of specialized rooms inside the giant, hollowed-out tree that was Owlboy's secret base of operations. Billy was attempting to explain his current predicament as they munched on snacks.

"There's really not all that much to understand," Billy said, trying to keep his voice calm. He was eating a cookie in the shape of a bat. "It's a special day once a year where kids dress up in costumes and go to people's houses asking for candy."

"And this works?" Halifax asked.

Billy nodded. "Most of the time. And if it doesn't, you play a trick on them."

"What kind of trick?" Archebold asked, pouring himself some poltergeist potion.

"I don't know." Billy shrugged. "I never had anybody not give me a treat before, though I hear that the tricks aren't all that bad. Y'know, like ringing the doorbell and running away, or throwing toilet paper in the trees. That kind of stuff."

He pulled a full tray of snacks closer, trying to decide what he wanted next. What he thought might be chocolate chips on a particular pastry were actually bugs that started to skitter off the tray, and were now trying to hide behind the jug of poltergeist potion.

"Sounds barbaric to me," Halifax said, brushing the crumbs from his banshee biscuit off the thick fur that hung from his face. "And while this is going on, costumes are being worn?"

"Yeah," Billy said, feeling his excitement spark. He loved Halloween—the smell in the air, the pumpkins, the scary decorations, the costumes. "You can be whatever you want on Halloween night, but most people pick something really scary. I'm surprised you guys don't have anything like it here in Monstros."

Archebold and Halifax looked at each other, a little confused.

"It's sort of scary here every night," Archebold explained. "What's the point?"

"I guess," Billy agreed. "But it's still wicked fun . . . well, most of the time anyway."

Billy's eyes suddenly danced behind his goggles. "You guys have got to help me," he said, wiping crumbs off the tabletop onto the floor. From the corner of his eye, he watched a tiny, mouselike creature run out of the shadows to feast upon them.

"What can we do?" Halifax asked.

"You can help me come up with the coolest costume that ever existed."

"I don't know, Billy," Archebold said. "We're really kind of busy with the whole stopping the spread of evil thing, but . . ."

"We'll do it," Halifax said excitedly. "Let me get my sketch pad and we'll start to brainstorm."

The troll approached a section of wall where there suddenly seemed to be a door. Billy didn't remember ever seeing one there, but Halifax walked through it anyway, disappearing into a darkened room only to appear seconds later holding a large pad of paper. He sat down next to Archebold.

"First, let's start with anything you *don't* want," the troll said.

"No monkeys in tutus," Billy stressed.

Archebold and Halifax looked at each other again.

"Whatever you say, boss." Archebold rolled his eyes.

"I just want you guys to give me some ideas," Billy continued, ignoring the looks. "I need to come up with something that nobody's ever seen before. That way I'm sure to win the contest."

"I've got it!" Halifax suddenly exclaimed. "This'll be great." He began to draw furiously. "Nobody up above has ever seen anything like this before," the troll said, drawing so fast that the movements of his pencil were practically a blur.

He finished and turned the pad toward Billy. "It's a Death-Bot 390."

Billy wasn't sure if he'd ever seen a robot so complicated, and so scary. It was actually too scary. "I don't know," he started to say.

"It'll be great," the troll interrupted. "Of course, we'll have to remove your brain and wire it into the robot's cybernetic nervous system."

"We'll probably have to do most of the building outside," Archebold added.

"Oh yeah, right," Halifax agreed. "The Death-Bot is over a hundred and fifty feet tall, and we only have a hundred-foot clearance in the workshop. Good thinking, Archebold."

"It's what I'm here for," the goblin said with a smile.

"Anyway," the troll went on, "we'll take your brain out, put it inside the cybernetic housing and then we'll get to work on the weapons systems. How do you feel about nuclear warheads?"

Billy's eyes practically exploded from behind his goggles. "Nuclear warheads?"

"Yeah, they'll give you candy for sure if you threaten to use one of those babies."

Archebold made an explosion sound, and he and Halifax started to laugh mischievously.

Billy felt a little creeped out.

"Y'know," he said, trying to be polite, "I don't think the Death-Bot 390 is what I'm looking for. How about something a little more Halloweeny . . . something more, well, more like a monster?"

The two monsters looked up from the elaborate drawing, clearly disappointed that Billy was rejecting the Death-Bot idea.

Halifax slowly flipped to a fresh page as Archebold muttered under his breath, stroking his chin in thought.

"I got it!" the goblin said with a snap of his fat, clawed fingers. "We won't even need to build anything for this one."

"What is it?" Halifax asked eagerly.

"Well, first we need to find the resting place of a Sumerian Revenge Demon," the goblin began.

"Go on," Halifax urged.

"We allow it to possess Billy, and then he'll be transformed into an ancient evil that hungers for the flesh and blood of the guilty."

"Brilliant!" Halifax shrieked, grabbing hold of Archebold's hand for a congratulatory handshake.

Billy was pretty much convinced that these two really didn't get the whole concept of Halloween, and he wasn't sure there was enough time in the next four centuries to explain it to them. *Death-Bots with nuclear warhead weapons systems? Sumerian Revenge Demons?*

He decided it was time to put a stop to this before things really got out of hand.

"Oh gosh, look at the time!" he exclaimed. He pulled up his sleeve and looked at his watch in mock surprise. "I really need to get going."

He jumped down from his chair.

"So should we start looking for the resting place of the Sumerian Revenge Demon?" Archebold asked.

"Yeah," Halifax added. "And remember, they're usually guarded by a small battalion of warrior mummies."

"Right," Archebold said. "We'll have to come up with the right offering to appease them. Warrior mummies are into scarab beetles, aren't they?"

Billy backed slowly toward the door.

"Why don't we put the brakes on the whole Sumerian Revenge Demon thing?" he suggested. "I've got a few ideas I've been working on back at the house."

"Better then transforming you into the embodiment of vengeance?" Halifax asked in disbelief.

"Yeah, I'm not too sure how my mom would feel about the whole transformation thing," Billy said.

The two creatures slowly nodded, but Billy could see by the looks on their faces that they really didn't understand.

"I'll let you know how the whole thing works out," he said as he opened the door to the hall.

"You sure you don't want to work on something here?" Archebold suggested. "Between the two of us, I'm sure we've got plenty more ideas."

"Nah, you two just go back to the whole combating evil thing and leave the Halloween stuff to me," Billy said with a wave, and then he was out the door.

It's a good thing they don't have Halloween here in Monstros, he thought to himself as he made his way toward the passage that would take him home.

I doubt anybody would survive the holiday.

CHAPTER 7

Billy climbed from the stone crypt and found his backpack where he'd hidden it in the corner. Jumpsuit, boots, gloves, goggles and helmet were quickly replaced by his jeans, sweatshirt and sneakers. Kneeling on the floor, he carefully folded up his costume, gathered his accessories and placed them inside his pack.

"Done and done," he muttered, zipping the bag and throwing it over his shoulder.

He was glad he'd decided to visit Monstros that morning; he had a much better attitude toward the task awaiting him. He was even beginning to think he might have a chance of pulling this off.

With a new confidence in his step, he opened the

mausoleum door and stepped out into the early-morning fall sunshine.

And nearly broke his neck tripping over the Big Wheel and the little girl astride it.

Victoria giggled uncontrollably. "You're funny, Billy," she said, tossing her head back as she continued to laugh.

"Oh yeah, I'm a real riot," Billy grumbled, sensing that a wrench, as well as a few screwdrivers, were about to be tossed into his plans for the day.

Victoria picked up the stuffed rabbit from where it was sitting on her lap. "Don't you think he's the funniest thing?" she asked Mr. Flops.

She placed her ear close to the rabbit's face, listening.

"He says you're wicked funny," she said with a smile and a slow nod.

"Great," Billy said sarcastically. "You have no idea how proud that makes me." He tried to get around her, but she quickly slid her bike into his path.

"We gonna play now?" she asked, her big blue eyes staring at him intently.

Billy's mind raced with possible options. He could tell her no, that he was too busy, which could result in a meltdown of Academy Award–winning proportions, and could very easily spin out of control when the

emotionally damaged child went looking for sympathy and found it from either her parents, or his.

He remembered the last time this had happened. He had the disturbing recollection of sitting at a tiny table in an equally tiny chair drinking imaginary tea with a gathering of baby dolls and stuffed animals, while Victoria happily sang a song she'd learned in school the previous day. The thought made him shiver uncontrollably.

"You said we'd play," the little girl whined, her lower lip already starting to tremble. "And I think I'll cry if we don't."

"Cancel the waterworks," he told her. "We're gonna do something even better than playing."

Victoria snatched up her stuffed rabbit and held it tight. "Did you hear that, Mr. Flops? We're gonna do something even funner than playing. What is it, Billy? What are we gonna do?"

"You, Victoria Grace McDevitt, are going to help me make the most spectacular Halloween costume ever created," he said excitedly.

The child was eerily quiet.

"I want to play grocery store," she finally said.

Billy shook his head enthusiastically. "No, don't you get it? You're gonna help me create a work of art."

Victoria thought again.

"You can be the checkout girl, and I'll be the customer," she said, her smile growing wider.

"No grocery store." Billy shook his head and waved his hands. "Get that right out of your head. It's Halloween costume or nothing."

Victoria sat back on her Big Wheel, Mr. Flops in her lap. She didn't look too thrilled as she gazed out over the cemetery.

"Whatcha gonna be?" she asked.

"Don't know," Billy answered, a fist-sized ball of nerves forming in his belly. "That's what we have to figure out. So, you ready?"

"I'm gonna be a princess," she announced with a smile.

"Great," he answered, starting to walk the path that would take them back to his yard.

"You could be a princess, too," Victoria suggested, pedaling her Big Wheel beside him.

"Don't be ridiculous," he said, sensing that his suggestion might not have been the brightest idea after all.

"You could be my sister."

"That's enough of that," he warned.

"Princess Billy," she added, and started to giggle.

Maybe he liked her better crying.

*   *   *

They stopped in front of the side door that would let them into the garage.

Billy looked down at the little girl. She had never been allowed inside before.

"Okay, before we go in, you have to promise me a few things," Billy began.

"What's that?" she asked.

"You have to promise not to reveal to anybody what you see inside this garage today."

"Not even my mom and dad?"

"Not even your mom and dad," Billy stressed. "What's inside here is top-secret."

"Top-secret," the little girl repeated, her eyes going to the door again. "I won't tell nobody."

"And you have to promise not to touch anything."

"Okay," she said, standing up, still straddling her Big Wheel and reaching for the old metal doorknob.

"Victoria!" Billy yelled.

The little girl jumped, pulling back her hand as if she'd been zapped with electricity. "What?" she asked.

"You have to promise me you're not going to touch anything."

Victoria nodded, her pigtails bouncing at the sides of her little head. "I promise not to touch anything," she said. "Now can we go in?"

There was a brief instant when Billy felt he was

making a huge mistake as he retrieved the key to the door, which was hidden over the doorframe.

"You promise?" Billy asked again, and the little girl nodded, bobbing her head up and down very fast.

"Yup."

He slipped the key into the lock and pushed the door. It squeaked eerily as it slowly swung open, and all he could think about were the countless haunted houses and mad scientists' laboratories that had been entered through squeaky doors just like this one in all the horror movies he'd seen.

Billy stepped into the darkened room, turning to see Victoria still standing at the entrance. "You coming in or not?" he asked.

"Don't you got any lights in here?"

"Sure I got lights," he answered, taking his backpack off and sticking it in a corner. There were a workstation and a table at the back of the garage and he carefully made his way toward them, careful not to trip over anything. He reached up for the pull chain that would turn on the ceiling lights. "Gotcha," he said, feeling the chain slip into his hands. He gave it a pull, illuminating the inside of the garage.

His workshop.

"Wow, look at all the junk!" Victoria squealed, darting inside.

"Be careful!" Billy yelled.

Victoria froze, Mr. Flops in her arms. "What is all this stuff?" she asked as her eyes moved about the room.

Billy leaned back against the worktable and crossed his arms. "Top-secret inventions that I've been working on over the years," he said proudly, his own eyes roving over his many accomplishments.

Victoria was on the move again. "What's this?" she asked, pointing to a contraption that had once been an old tricycle, a washing machine motor and six digital clocks all flashing 12:00.

"That's my time machine," Billy said matter-of-factly.

"Does it work?" Victoria asked.

"Nah, I can't get the clocks to stop flashing twelve, but I think I might be getting close."

She approached another invention—two old-fashioned fire extinguishers and a battered life preserver. The two extinguishers had been bound to the life preserver with electrical tape.

"This looks interesting," she said, slowly reaching out to touch it.

He should have known she couldn't resist, and intercepted her hand. "That's my jetpack prototype," he explained. "Once I get it working, I'll be able to fly to school."

Victoria's eyes bugged out.

"Wow. Will you make me one so I can fly to school, too?" the little girl asked.

"You don't go to school," Billy said, rolling his eyes. "Kindergarten doesn't really count."

"It does too!" Victoria screeched, stamping her foot. "We have to take naps and everything."

"All right, all right," he said. "Don't get your Underoos in a bunch."

She had already wandered off toward a section of the garage that had a Captain Saturn and the Galactic Rangers sheet spread across it. Billy hurried to catch up with her.

"What's behind here?" she asked, reaching to lift the sheet up.

Billy stepped in front of her, his back to the sheet. "There's nothing behind here for you. Let's go over there and I'll show you my design for rocket shoes."

"Why can't I see what's behind this sheet?" she said, trying to get around him.

"It's just junk back there, you wouldn't have any interest in . . ."

She was fast, he had to give her that. Victoria dropped to the floor like a weasel and crawled beneath the sheet.

"No!" Billy yelped, reaching down to grab the makeshift curtain. As he emerged on the other side, he saw the little girl standing before the large table his father had built him when he was just a little kid, staring in awe at his elaborate constructions.

When he was little, Billy had loved Constructo building blocks—no, it was more than that; he'd been obsessed with them. He had built everything from skyscrapers to airplanes to space shuttles. And as he'd built them, he had put them away, refusing to break them apart. Eventually, there hadn't been any more space inside his room, and his father had made him this special table to display all his Constructo creations.

He loved these things that he'd built with his own two hands.

And Victoria was reaching out to touch them.

"*Yeeeeeeeeeeeek!*" Billy screamed, diving for the little girl before her hand could reach his Constructo-block version of the Chrysler Building.

But he was too late. Her little fingers gently brushed the side of the building.

Billy froze, holding his breath. "Back away slowly," he whispered.

"Did you build these, Billy?" Victoria asked, ignoring his order.

He nodded, gesturing for her to come toward him. "Yeah, I did. Would you come over here, please?"

"Why?" the little girl asked. "I'm not gonna break nothing. I just want to look some more."

She turned back to the table.

Just then, the Chrysler Building began to tip.

It was like something out of a giant monster movie. Victoria stood before the display as the building fell over, knocking down a Constructo plane hanging by wires from the ceiling, which then fell on an elaborate Constructo bridge and collapsed on top of a Constructo ship.

And so on and so on.

It was like watching the end of the world.

One by one, Billy's favorite childhood memories crumbled into multicolored plastic rubble.

Slowly he turned his eyes to *her*.

The destroyer.

"Whoops," Victoria said, squeezing Mr. Flops tightly in her arms. "How the heck did that happen?"

His anger was like a volcano. Billy could feel it building up inside him, rumbling and grumbling until he couldn't hold it back any longer.

"How did it happen?" he asked, approaching the table. He picked up a piece of what used to be a Constructo block 747. "You touched it, that's how it happened!"

Victoria's eyes started to blink and he could see the tears beginning to form, but he was so angry he didn't care.

"I'm sorry. Here." She held out Mr. Flops. "Give him a hug and I bet you feel better."

Billy wanted to rip Mr. Flops' head off and eat it. "I can't believe I trusted you," he said, shaking his head. "I should've known you'd use your . . . your Destructo Touch on something!"

"I don't have a Destructo Touch!" Victoria screamed. "It was an accident!"

"But what about all the other times?" Billy cried. "What about my remote-control racecar? What about my karaoke machine? And my Mr. Slushy Summertime Treat Maker?" Then, wearing his meanest face, he pointed at her. "You have the Destructo Touch."

And with those words, Victoria started to cry.

"You're a meany, Billy Hooten!" she screamed through her tears, and clutching Mr. Flops, she crawled under the sheet and was gone.

"Good riddance," Billy hollered, but even as he looked at the enormous pile of Constructo blocks that used to be something, he could feel the first twinges of guilt.

Somehow he was going to pay for making Victoria cry, he knew that for sure.

Victoria didn't know why she ran into the cemetery, but she did.

She snuffled, wiping her nose on the sleeve of her jacket as she leaned back against the big old oak tree.

"Billy Hooten is the stupidest stupid-head," she cried, big tears rolling down her cheeks.

She hugged Mr. Flops, burying her face in the softness of his fur. "You don't think I have the Destructo Touch, do you?" she asked the stuffed bunny.

Holding him out before her, she waited for his reply.

"I don't think so, either," she said, sitting down on the exposed roots of the old oak tree. "It was just a little accident . . . they was all accidents. I don't know what he had to get so mad about."

She had managed to stop crying. The sadness of her bestest friend in the whole wide world yelling at her turned to anger.

As she looked around the cemetery, her eyes fell upon the old stone mausoleum. Earlier that morning, she had followed Billy into the cemetery and watched as he had gone inside the spooky stone building.

"I wonder what he was doing in there?" she asked Mr. Flops. He hadn't stayed in there very long. Victoria's curiosity began to grow.

"Maybe he hided something," she suggested to the rabbit. "Something he didn't want to share."

The little girl scowled. "Not only is he a big stupid-head, he's a big stupid-head who doesn't know how to share."

Victoria got up from where she was sitting and wiped some loose leaves from her butt, never taking her eyes off the mausoleum. "I wonder if it's candy," she said aloud. "Or maybe even a new toy."

She walked across the lawn, between the rows of headstones, toward the mausoleum. *He probably hid it in here because it's kinda scary looking,* she thought as she approached the building, but she wasn't scared.

Her mind danced with all the things she imagined Billy might have hid inside the small building—everything from Gummy Bears to a brand-new Baby Poop and Burp doll.

Victoria hoped he had hid a Baby Poop and Burp; she wanted to play with one of them wicked bad.

With a grunt, she pushed open the metal door and stood just inside the doorway. She looked around the dusty room, wondering where Billy might've hidden his treasure, and decided to enter the mausoleum for a closer look.

"So where do you think he hid the stuff?" she asked Mr. Flops. She noticed that the lid on one of the stone coffins at the far end of the room was slightly ajar, and moved toward it.

"Yeah, that cover does look sorta crooked. My thinking exactly, Mr. Flops."

She climbed onto the platform where the coffin rested and stood on her tippy-toes to try and look down into the darkness within. She could barely see over the edge.

"You think a Baby Poop and Burp might be in there?" she asked her stuffed companion. "Sure is dark, though. Don't know if I want to go inside there."

An echo of her voice reverberated up from within the stone coffin, scaring her at first—but then she found it sort of cool.

"Hello down there!" she called.

Hello down there, it echoed back.

She started to laugh. "That's creepy," she said between giggles.

Victoria continued to sit at the stone coffin's edge, the tips of her sneakers dangling down into the pitch black.

"I think I've changed my mind," she said, turning so that she could jump down to the floor from the edge. "I'm not gonna go in."

But as she turned around, the side of her foot hit Mr. Flops, and the rabbit pitched forward into the coffin. Into the darkness.

"Mr. Flops, what're you doing?" Victoria screamed. And without a second's hesitation, she spun back around and hopped inside after her stuffed friend.

She had no choice but to follow.

CHAPTER 8

Archebold's single, monocled eyeball—magnified to three times its normal size casually scanned *Celebrity Creature* magazine. Licking a stubby finger, he turned the page of the latest issue of monster gossip.

"We should get Billy mentioned in here," Archebold said, flipping through the next few pages.

He and Halifax were in a chamber designated the Rest Room, and were doing just that. Resting.

The room was filled to the gills with all kinds of comfortable chairs and couches, most so overstuffed that sitting on them felt like resting on a cloud.

"What's that?" Halifax asked sleepily, rolling over to face the goblin.

"In here," Archebold squeaked, waving the magazine at the troll. "We should get them to do a story on the new Owlboy. It would be great publicity."

Halifax reached into the top front pocket of his overalls and removed a cellophane bag. "I don't think questions about what his favorite color is and what kind of animal he'd like to be would help with striking fear into the hearts of evildoers," the furry creature said, opening the bag. "Scab?" he asked, offering the bag to Archebold.

"I guess you're right." Archebold glanced up from his magazine. "Are those Flaky Frank Scabs?" he asked.

Halifax read the label on the bag. "Yeah, barbecue flavor."

The goblin shook his head. "No thanks, I only eat Leprous Louie's All-Natural Scabs."

"Fussbudget," Halifax growled through a mouthful of barbecue-flavored scabs.

Suddenly alarm bells began to chime, disturbing the peaceful quiet of the Rest Room.

"Which one is that?" Archebold asked, putting a stubby finger in one of his prominent ears to dull the clamor.

There were alarms for everything at the Roost: alarms for when it started to rain, and for when it stopped; alarms for when it was time to put the trash out; and even alarms for when it was time for Halifax to change his overalls.

That alarm usually couldn't come fast enough.

"Something's getting too close to the Roost," the troll said, digging into the empty bag for crumbs. "Probably just some nosy varmint . . . maybe you should go check?"

Archebold looked up from his magazine and seriously thought about it. "Nah. Maybe you should, though?"

The troll folded the empty scabs bag on his belly.

"Or we could just activate that new automatic security system I installed this week?"

"Excellent idea," Archebold said.

"I thought so," Halifax agreed, pulling a remote control with an extralong antenna from inside his front overall pocket.

"We're too busy," the goblin said with a throaty chuckle, finding a recipe for Bloodberry Pie inside his magazine which he started to tear out to save. Maybe he would make it over the weekend.

"You got that right," Halifax agreed, pushing the button on the remote to activate the new security system.

"Too busy to sweat the small stuff."

* * *

"Any clue where you're going, oh great hunter?" Sireena called after her brother as the two of them continued to push their way through the Wailing Wood.

"I thought I saw something moving up here," Sigmund grunted. "It's probably *him*, cowering in fear, tired and frightened because he hasn't the strength to run from us any longer."

"Or it could be your eyes playing tricks on you," Sireena said, wiping a strand of spiderweb from her face.

They had been hunting Owlboy for quite some time now, and still were no closer to finding him.

Distracted by the sounds of the woods, Sireena didn't notice that her brother had come to a stop and plowed into his back, the muzzle of her rifle poking him in his big behind.

"Yeeek!" Sigmund squealed. He spun around, violence in his bugging eyes.

"You did that on purpose," he snarled.

"I didn't know you'd stopped," Sireena said in her defense. "Why did you stop?"

"Because I think I know where he's hiding," her sibling said, and he pointed with his gun to a fantastic tree.

"Now that's a big tree," Sireena said, stepping around her brother to get a better look. The tree was enormous, quite possibly the biggest tree she had ever seen in her entire life.

"As good a place as any to hide from us, eh, good sister?" Sigmund said, nudging her with the butt of his rifle. He moved stealthily closer to the base of the tree and the huge roots that had pushed up from the ground.

The evil troll stood between a large passage left on either side of two of the great cords of root, peering into a dark opening that seemed to lead into the base.

"*He* could be hiding in there," Sigmund said, doing his best to see beyond the veil of black.

"*Hoo!*" rang out a voice.

Sigmund spun around and growled at his sister. "You know exactly who I'm talking about. Don't start."

"I didn't say a thing," Sireena answered, raising her weapon and looking around.

"*Hoo!*" said the voice again.

Sigmund stepped closer to the yawning darkness of the opening in the base of the tree. "I think it might've come from in here," he said. He held his rifle at the ready. "Maybe it's *him*."

"*Hoo! Hoo! Hoo! Hoo!*" The closer he got, the more *hoos* there were.

"I think there's more than one of him," Sigmund said, his eyes wide with anticipation as he looked away from the trunk opening.

And then there came the sound—the flapping of wings—and within the darkness multiple sets of round, piercing yellow eyes became illuminated.

"*Hoo! Hoo! Hoo! Hoo! Hoo! Hoo!*"

"I think you might want to get away from there," Sireena suggested, slowly starting to back away from the clearing.

"I think that might be a good idea," Sigmund answered.

And just as her brother turned, ready to join her, they exploded from the darkness.

"*Hoo! Hoo! Hoo! Hoo! Hoo! Hoo! Hoo! Hoo! Hoo!*"

Mechanical birds, hundreds of them, spewed out from the tree, their hooting hollers nearly deafening.

Back to back, Sireena and her brother raised their weapons, firing wildly at the clockwork creatures that swarmed around their heads. The mechanical birds exploded with each shot, a rain of springs, cogs, metal feathers and wires pelting down on them. But for each bird that was destroyed by one of their weapons' blasts, another three seemed to take its place.

"This is hopeless," Sireena bellowed.

"*Hoo! Hoo! Hoo! Hoo! Hoo! Hoo! Hoo! Hoo!*"

"I agree," her sibling responded, probably one of the first times he'd ever agreed with her.

"How would you feel about fleeing in terror?" she said.

"I thought you'd never ask," Sigmund responded, already plowing head-on into the Wailing Wood.

"*Hoo! Hoo! Hoo! Hoo! Hoo! Hoo! Hoo! Hoo!*"

The stone coffin didn't seem to have a bottom.

Victoria tumbled through the darkness—down, down, down she went—but before she could be afraid, she found herself finally hitting bottom.

It took her a moment to realize that she had stopped falling, and that she had landed on something kind of soft and squishy, like a pillow.

"Hey, get off me. You're breaking my back!" a squeaky voice complained.

"Who's that?" Victoria asked, trying to see who was talking to her in this incredibly dark place.

"Down here," the voice answered as somebody lit a match, chasing away some of the darkness.

Victoria looked down and saw that she had landed on Mr. Flops. The rabbit looked up at her, trapped, holding a wooden match that looked like a torch in his hands.

"Mr. Flops?" she asked. "Is that you?"

"Well, it ain't Baby Poop and Burp," the stuffed rabbit said. "Would you mind getting off me?"

"Sorry," Victoria said, scrambling to her feet.

"That's better," the rabbit said, picking himself up from the ground and dusting off his gray fur.

"You can talk and move around?" Victoria asked.

The rabbit brought the matchstick torch down and

checked himself out, doing a little dance step. "Yeah, would ya look at that? I guess I can."

"My mommy says it's not good to play with matches," the little girl said.

"Give me a sec," he said, and blew the match out with a gust of his breath, plunging the area in darkness again.

"Mr. Flops?" Victoria called out.

Another light was suddenly lit, much brighter than the match.

"How's this?" the rabbit asked, now holding a flashlight.

"Great," she said. "Where did you get a flashlight?"

"From my pocket," Mr. Flops answered. He reached inside his fur and removed another flashlight. "Want one?"

"Sure," Victoria said, taking the light and turning it on. "I didn't even know you had pockets."

The rabbit shone his flashlight around the dark chamber where they stood. "Neither did I," Mr. Flops said. "Any idea where we are?"

Victoria copied her friend, moving her beam of light around in a circle. "I think we might be under the cemetery," she said.

"Wherever we are, it sure is dark."

"Yeah, and kind of spooky."

"Are you afraid?" Mr. Flops asked.

"Nah," Victoria answered. "I like spooky stuff. Are you scared?"

She felt the rabbit's furry soft paw grab hold of her hand. "Not as long as you're with me," he said, and gave her the cutest bunny smile.

"I wonder where all these go?" Victoria shone her flashlight across the openings to passages that led off in different directions into the darkness.

"Maybe one of them can get us back up to the cemetery," Mr. Flops said.

Victoria was just about to suggest that they explore when she heard the weirdest of sounds: somebody—two somebodies, by the sound of it—was screaming.

Victoria looked at Mr. Flops.

"Sounds like somebody's in trouble," the rabbit said.

"Yeah," she agreed. "Do you think we should help them?"

The rabbit was silent for a bit as the two of them listened to the ruckus off in the distance.

"Maybe if we help whoever that is, they can tell us how to get back up to the cemetery," Mr. Flops said.

"That sounds like a good idea," Victoria agreed. And still holding the rabbit's hand, she walked toward one of the dark passages.

CHAPTER 9

The mechanical owls were still in hot pursuit, their hooting a sound so chilling that Sigmund Sassafras would be hearing it in his nightmares for years to come.

"Do you see the van yet?" his sister screamed over the hooting.

"Not yet," he called over his shoulder, raising his rifle to swat at a clockwork bird pecking on the top of his head. "But I think we're getting warmer."

This section of woods was packed tightly with trees barren of leaves, their empty branches trailing down like skeletal hands.

"Remind me again why I listened to you?" Sireena wailed behind him, the low-hanging tree limbs catching in her hair.

Sigmund was tempted to leave her behind and let the owls have at her, but he knew he'd never be able to explain it to his mother. Even through the glass partition in the prison visiting room, she could sense a lie as easily as a V'larkian Sucking Toad could sniff out a fresh chicken neck in a blizzard of locusts.

Sireena was still caught up in the tree's clinging branches, most of the owl flock flying around her.

"*Hoo! Hoo! Hoo! Hoo! Hoo! Hoo! Hoo! Hoo! Hoo!*"

"Hold still," Sigmund yelled, leveling his weapon. He fired three blasts in a row that turned the tree into toothpicks and sent Sireena flying in a plume of fire.

The air was choked with smoke, and suddenly eerily quiet.

"Sireena?" Sigmund waved at the smoke billowing around him. He was beginning to worry that he might have overdone it. "If you can hear me, say something . . . anything."

"You idiot!" growled an all-too-familiar voice.

Sireena emerged from the choking cloud, her clothing torn and covered with black smudges of ash. "Look at me!" she screamed. "Look at my clothes . . . my makeup! You tried to kill me!"

"If I had wanted to kill you, you'd be dead." Sigmund reached out to take her by a dirty sleeve. "We need to find the van and . . ."

There was a loud ripping sound as the sleeve came away in his hand.

"Whoops," he said with a nervous laugh, quickly hiding the piece of shirt behind his back.

That was when Sireena lost it. Growling like a rabid garganturat, she jumped on him and tried to tear his head from his shoulders. The two thrashed on the forest floor, the nine hundred and ninety-ninth time they'd tried to kill each other. But as the smoke from the rifle blasts began to clear, Sigmund noticed—felt—that they weren't alone in the Wailing Wood.

"Wait a minute!" he croaked, his voice sounding high and squeaky with his sister's hands wrapped so tightly around his throat. "I think we're being watched."

Sireena stopped trying to strangle him and looked around, giving him the chance to crawl out from beneath her.

The branches of the trees surrounding them were filled with glowing yellow eyes. The mechnical owls had not left them alone after all; they had only stopped to watch as the two siblings tried to murder each other.

"I told you." Sigmund elbowed his sister in the ribs.

Sireena grunted, raising her fist to pummel him again, but stopped midstrike as the birds stirred with a fluttering of metal wings.

"I wouldn't do that if I were you," Sigmund said quietly.

Sireena lowered her fist slowly. "What do you think they're waiting for?" she asked through the side of her extra-wide mouth.

"I don't know," Sigmund replied as he began to back away. "But I don't intend to stick around to find out."

And suddenly he was off and running, heading (he hoped) in the direction of the van. He could hear Sireena huffing and puffing behind him, but he could also hear the sound of metal wings flapping.

The owls were after them again, and if the entrance to the woods, with the van parked outside it, wasn't right ahead, he knew they weren't going to make it.

The birds were closer now. He could hear the grinding of their cogs and gears.

It was Sireena who put the final nail in their coffin. She stumbled, falling forward and getting tangled in his legs, sending them both sprawling to the ground in a grunting heap.

"And I'm the idiot," Sigmund whined, crawling to his feet only to find two terrifying new creatures standing before him.

"Hello, Mr. Idiot." The greeting came from a ghastly creature with a round, pink face and hair like antenna sticking out from the sides of its head.

"I'm Mr. Flops," said the other, smaller beast with the disturbingly long ears and the body covered in gray fur. "And this is Victoria."

"Eeeeeeeeeeeeek!" Sireena screamed, grabbing hold of Sigmund in a grip that would make a boa constrictor proud. "What are they?"

"I . . . I don't know," Sigmund wheezed, feeling the life being squeezed from him. "They say they are a Mr. Flops and something called Victoria."

But then the birds were upon them, hooting and pecking, and Sigmund, still held in the clutches of his sister, could do nothing more than close his eyes and accept whatever grisly fate was about to befall them. At least he wasn't going to perish alone.

But suddenly it was silent.

Sigmund opened his eyes a crack. The mechanized birds were lying on the ground in pieces, as if some powerful force had plucked them out of the air and crushed them to dust.

"Wha . . . what happened?" Sireena asked, opening her own eyes.

"I didn't think they were very nice," the creature called Victoria said. Mr. Flops nodded.

"What did you do?" Sigmund asked, kicking at the owl pieces with a toe.

"I touched 'em," the creature said proudly, holding

out her tiny pink hands. "Billy says I got the Destructo Touch."

"Yes, you certainly do," Sigmund agreed, his criminally active mind already beginning to formulate a plan.

"You do indeed."

No matter how hard he tried to distract himself, Billy was still feeling guilty about yelling at Victoria.

Now he sat at the worktable, wads of crinkled-up paper nearly covering his feet. He thought he might have something with this latest attempt, mixing a bit of the squid creatures from the Monstros City savings and loan with a kind of prehistoric lizard.

A squizard! he thought. *Nobody's seen one of them before.*

He finished drawing the last of the tentacles and leaned back, taking in the drawing.

"What a load of garbage," he snarled, wrinkling up the paper and tossing it to the floor with the others.

He was about to start his next drawing, but all he could see in his mind was Victoria's face twisting all out of shape as she started to cry. He rubbed at his eyes, trying to get the pathetic image out of his brain.

But it wasn't going anywhere.

Billy sighed and put his glasses back on. He knew he wasn't going to get anything more accomplished until he'd apologized to Victoria and made her feel better. Rising from the bench, he set his pencil down so that it wouldn't roll off the table, and waded through the pieces of paper toward the garage door.

He knew there'd probably be a price to pay, and wondered how many weeks he'd have to play "grocery store checkout" or "superheroes buy a bike" before she'd let him off the hook.

Walking across the floor, he felt the bottom of one of his sneakers stick. "What the ...?" he said aloud, noticing a large puddle of white paint on the concrete. *Victoria must have knocked over the can on her way out,* he thought. Then he noticed the little sneaker footprints that made their way toward the partially open door.

"Oh, man," Billy said with a shake of his head. Now he was going to have to clean that up too.

Careful not to step in the paint, he left the garage and followed Victoria's trail. Her Big Wheel was still parked in front of the door, and he expected to see the white prints go across his driveway toward her house, but they didn't.

Instead the trail went through the backyard, white paint shining brightly on the fall grass. "This is odd," Billy said as he checked the top of the stone wall that separated the yard from the cemetery. There was white paint there, too.

He scrambled over the wall and down into the cemetery. The paint had obviously begun to wear off her sneakers, but he still found enough traces to follow.

He started to get a nasty feeling in the pit of his belly. Of all places, the white-stained blades of grass led right to the Sprylock family mausoleum. Which just happened to be the entrance to Monstros City.

He thought he just might die.

"Maybe she went in, got scared and went home," Billy muttered under his breath, hoping with all his heart and soul that that was what had happened.

Pushing open the door, he entered the mausoleum and looked around. It was unmistakable: the fading tread marks led right up to the stone coffin and the entrance to Monstros City.

Billy ran to the edge of the coffin and peered down into the impenetrable darkness. "This is horrible," he muttered crazily. "This is the worst thing ever."

He could feel himself beginning to panic. For a moment he considered running home and calling 911, but quickly got a grip. "Yeah, that'd be real good. '911, what is your emergency?' Ah, my five-year-old next-door neighbor climbed into a coffin in the Sprylock family mausoleum and is now in a city of monsters. When do you think you can get here?'"

Billy stepped back from the coffin. "All right, Hooten, nobody else can help you with this one. So, what's it gonna be?"

And without another thought, he bolted from the mausoleum.

He had to get his costume.

This looked like a job for Owlboy.

Billy went over the cemetery wall and into his yard.

He practically flew across the lawn, but as he neared the garage, he saw his mother at the back door with a UPS delivery man who was handing her a large, brown-wrapped box.

His curiosity aroused, Billy almost stopped to check it out, but quickly pushed the idea from his head. He had to rescue Victoria from Monstros.

"Hey, honey, wait up!" he heard his mother cry just as he opened the door to the garage.

Billy sighed. If only he'd been a little bit faster! "Hey, Mom, sort of busy," he yelled, and ducked inside, slamming the door behind him. He hoped she would get the hint as he crossed the room and snatched up his backpack from the floor.

But, alas, the door opened and in she walked, still holding the mystery package. "Hey, kid," she said, a big smile on her face.

He returned the smile, trying to maneuver around her and out the door. "Got an important engagement," he said. "Gotta go, talk to you later."

But she blocked his way.

"Now, wait a second," she said. "Don't tell me you're not curious about what's inside this box."

The image of Victoria being chased by a Sludge Slogger—or even worse, a Slovakian Rot-toothed Hopping Monkey Demon—flashed before Billy's eyes.

"Yeah, I am, but I really got to get going! It's wicked important."

His mom looked down at the box and sighed. He thought she looked kind of disappointed, and felt a surge of regret. He'd make it up to her later.

"All right," she said, moving out of his way and placing the box on the worktable. "Just thought you might like to know that your Halloween costume problem is solved."

He was just about to disappear out the door when he slammed on the brakes. "My Halloween costume?" he asked, turning around to face her.

She was looking at her fingernails, playing it cool.

"Did I say something about a Halloween costume?" she asked. "Oh, this?" she said, pointing at the box on the table. "Yeah, this could very well be the answer to all your problems."

He was amazed. Normally his mother couldn't re-member anything; the fact that she'd recalled he was having difficulty with his Halloween costume was nearly a miracle.

Billy started toward her, but stopped. There was still Victoria to worry about.

"Oh, go on." His mother waved him away. She smiled, leaning on the large box. "This'll still be here when you get back."

Billy didn't want to go, but there wasn't any choice.

Victoria needed him.

CHAPTER 10

The alarm was even louder than the fire alarm at school, and that was enough to make Billy's ears bleed.

He reached the door at the end of the dark passage. Using the special owlhead key Archebold had given him, he let himself into the Roost. The door opened into the Roost's observation room, and it appeared to be in total chaos. The clanging alarm seemed to be even louder in here, and Archebold and Halifax were running around in what seemed to be a total panic.

"What's with that racket?" he asked, putting the funky key into a pocket on his utility belt.

Archebold was standing by an ancient printer which was spewing out reams of paper. "Thank goodness you're here," he said, looking up. "The city is in turmoil."

"It's terrible," Halifax said from where he stood. Multiple old television sets were stacked, row after row, from floor to ceiling, behind him. He was holding a remote control in one of his furry hands.

"What's happening?" Billy asked.

"All over the city," Halifax grumbled, never taking his eyes from the screens. "It's chaos."

Billy had to agree. Everywhere he looked he saw scenes of destruction. Buildings had toppled into rubble; cars were burning; there was panic in the streets as the citizens of Monstros hopped, flew, slithered and skittered to safety.

"What did this?" Billy asked, looking away from the TV screens.

"Every report says the same thing," Archebold replied, holding the latest information up to his monocle-covered eye. "Things were fine, and then suddenly everything went crazy. Something bad has come to Monstros City, Billy. Something really bad."

Billy was about to ask what he should do, when he caught himself. He was Owlboy; it was up to *him* to figure it out. Victoria would have to wait until the city was safe.

"Do we have any clues at all?" he asked, looking

back at the different screens. "What's up with the destroyed buildings?" He stepped closer to the sets for a better look. "Hey, wait a minute—Monstros City Savings and Loan, Five Coffin Savings, Vampire National—these are all banks!"

Archebold dug through the printouts. "Yeah, you're right."

"I sense criminal activity." Billy stroked his chin with a gloved hand. "Are there any witnesses?"

"It says here that the police are questioning eye-witnesses at the Monstros City police headquarters," Archebold said, waving one of the printouts.

"So that's where we need to go," Billy decided.

Archebold dropped the printouts, while still more continued to flow from the machine. "Very good, sir."

"Halifax, you stay here and continue to monitor the situation," Billy instructed the troll.

"Right," Halifax responded with a salute.

Billy spun around, feeling his feathered cape flow behind him as he headed for the door that would take him to the Roost's garage. What he said next was something he'd been waiting to say since first putting on the costume of the mysterious crime fighter.

And the words were just as exciting as he imagined they would be.

"To the Owlmobile, Archebold!"

Then he dashed from the room.

*　*　*

Rubber boots squeaking as he came to a stop in front of the vehicle storage garage, Billy headed for the Owl-mobile.

Archebold had just caught up, searching for his keys as he slid to a stop on the driver's side, when a voice from the loudspeaker interrupted them.

"Excuse me," Halifax said. "Just got a look at the traffic report, and you're not getting anywhere anytime soon. The city's tied up in knots."

Archebold stamped his foot. "I should've thought of that," he grumbled. He ducked inside the car and pulled a map from the glove compartment. "Maybe I can find a way around the chaos." He spread the map across the top of the hood and placed his monocle over his right eye.

"Let's see." The goblin began to study the intricate multicolored squiggles that represented the city's elaborate road system.

The map made Billy's eyes cross, so instead he focused on the machines parked around the garage. There were trucks of all sizes and shapes, as well as motorcycles, and something else that squatted in the far corner. Even though it was partially hidden by a tarp, he could still make out what it was, and knew that it was the best solution to their current predicament.

"Hey, Archebold," Billy said.

"I'm very busy here, sir," the goblin answered. "I need complete concentration so that—"

"Who said we had to drive?" Billy said.

"Excuse me?"

But Billy was already crossing the room to the covered vehicle. "Who said we had to drive?" he repeated, grabbing handfuls of the tarp and pulling them away to reveal a bright yellow helicopter in the same bird's-head design as the Owlmobile.

"When we could fly."

Archebold smiled and started to fold up the map.

"Oh yeah, I forgot we had one of those."

The Owlcopter swooped low over the city.

"It's awful," Billy said, face pressed to the bubble glass of the craft's tinted windshield. "It's like something carved a path of destruction through the streets. But what coulda done it?"

"That's what we've got to figure out," Archebold said, piloting the humming craft through a plume of thick black smoke that snaked up from a burning building below them. "Before this gets any worse."

The copter suddenly leaned to the left, and began to quickly descend.

"Hold onto your intestines," Archebold announced. "I'm putting her down on the roof of police headquarters."

He landed the Owlcopter with little difficulty, and without a second's hesitation, they hit the stairs, descending into the station.

Billy went through the door first, entering into a sea of confusion.

"It's just as bad in here," Archebold observed.

The station was filled to the gills with every kind of creature imaginable, all of them attempting to speak at the same time. The police officers were doing their best to listen, but it was just too much.

Billy looked around, certain that somewhere inside the room there was somebody—or something; he was in Monstros, after all—that could help them put a stop to whatever was responsible for the devastation in the city.

Bringing a hand to his mouth, Billy coughed loudly once, and then again. It was on the third try, when he added an equally loud throat clearing, that he finally got their attention.

They were all very freaky, but what did he expect in a city of monsters? *Sports Illustrated* swimsuit models?

"Say something," Archebold whispered out of the corner of his mouth, elbowing him in the side.

"Hey there." Billy gave them all a little wave. "Pretty crazy out there, huh?"

A white-furred beast wearing a very ugly Hawaiian shirt, shorts and sandals was the first to speak. "It's him," he growled. "It's Owlboy."

And it started to spread like wildfire; each of the ghouls, ghosties and long-legged beasties repeating his name as they all began to realize who he was.

"Quiet!" ordered a voice that sounded like mountains being smashed.

The squeaks, shrieks, buzzings and clickings immediately fell silent, and this time all eyes, including Billy's, who had to climb on top of a desk in order to see, turned to the back of the room and fell upon Chief Bloodwart, standing outside his office. The chief looked as though he'd been chiseled from a piece of solid rock, his large body full of angles so sharp that they threatened to tear through the material of his dark blue police officer's uniform.

"It's bad enough that I've got chaos in the streets, I'm not going to have it in here. Do I make myself clear?"

The creatures quieted down.

"Hey, Chief!" Billy called out, waving from atop the desk.

"Well, well," Chief Bloodwart rumbled. He walked

across the room, his footfalls like little bolts of thunder. "If it isn't our newest Owlboy." He stopped before the desk, eye level with Billy. "I've been hearing lots of good things about you."

"Thanks, Chief," Billy answered, feeling himself blush. "I'm just trying to do my best."

The rock creature slowly nodded. "And with that attitude, it seems to me that you're on the right track."

Archebold elbowed Billy's side. "Ask him about the witnesses."

"Oh yeah." Billy looked back at the police chief, doing his best to give off an air of authority. "I was wondering if you could use my help with your current situation."

The chief rubbed a stony hand across his chiseled jaw; it sounded like sandpaper rubbing on concrete. "Me and some of my officers have already talked to a few witnesses, but we didn't really get all that much information other than one minute everything was fine, and the next everything went kablooey."

"That kablooey is a problem," Billy said knowingly.

"I was just about to question the last of them," Bloodwart said. "If you'd like to take a crack, be my guest."

Billy hopped down from the desk.

Chief Bloodwart stared down at him, tiny pinpricks

of red glowing from deep within cavelike eye sockets. "You seriously think you might be able to help?"

"I'll do my best," Billy answered, crossing his arms and puffing out his chest.

The chief started to laugh—a weird sound, like rocks being dropped on piles of spaghetti. "I bet you will," he said, walking back through the still quiet crowd.

Billy and Archebold followed the chief, and Billy could feel the eyes of those gathered in the station house staring as he passed.

"Do you think he can do it?" he heard one of the citizens ask. "He does seem sorta young."

"I don't know what it is, but I think the kid has something going for him," said another of the monsters. "If he was running for mayor, I'd vote for him."

"I think he's kind of cute. Wonder if he's married," said a voice whose words made Billy blush again.

"Guess I've got a way with the ladies, eh, Archebold?" Billy said to his companion, an extra bit of macho swagger in his step.

Archebold glanced over his shoulder at the crowd. "Lady? If you say so."

Billy didn't want to ask, deciding to place all his focus on Chief Bloodwart, who had just opened the door to the interview room next to his office and was gesturing for them to enter.

The room was small, containing a single table. A giant spider with a drawing pad and pencils in each of its hands sat on one end of the table, and a really old-looking werewolf sat at the other end.

"Can I go home now?" the werewolf asked, fanged dentures suddenly flying out of his mouth and landing on top of the table. "Darn things," he grumbled, snatching up his teeth and shoving them back into his mouth.

"How are we doing?" Chief Bloodwart asked the spider.

"Not so good," the arachnid's high-pitched voice squeaked. "He says he doesn't want to think about it because it was too horrible."

Bloodwart then turned his attention to Billy. "This is our sketch artist, Bugsy," the chief explained. "He's been trying to get a description of our culprit from Mr. Lupo here . . . isn't that right, Mr. Lupo?"

The werewolf snarled, folding his spindly arms across his chest. "Don't want to talk about it anymore. I just want to get home and forget about the whole horrible thing. When you get to be my age, you can't deal with things the way you used to."

Lupo's teeth flew out again, but this time the old-timer caught them before they could hit the ground.

"Darn things," he growled again, moving them around before they slid into place.

The werewolf had the look of somebody who'd just

about had it, and wasn't about to do anything they didn't want to do. Billy had seen the look before, especially from his Aunt Tessie, who was wicked old too. Billy wracked his memory, trying to remember the trick of how his parents got Aunt Tessie to do what they wanted.

Suddenly it came to him.

"Excuse us," Billy said, taking Archebold by the arm and leading him into a corner.

"What'd I do?" the goblin asked, near panic in his voice.

"Nothing," Billy answered. "Do you have any candy on you?"

Archebold looked shocked at first, and then his eyes started to dart around, looking everywhere except at Billy.

"No . . . no, I don't have any candy . . . and . . . and if I did, I . . . I would certainly give you—"

"Knock it off," Billy barked. If there was one thing he'd learned about goblins, it was that the little green guys loved their treats. "I need a piece of candy if we're going to get Mr. Lupo to talk to us. Cough it up."

Archebold slumped. "Oh, all right," he grumbled. "But I was really looking forward to this cockroach crunch bar."

The goblin reached into his pocket and pulled out the candy, which Billy eagerly snatched. "Don't worry,

I'll buy you two of these later." He turned his attention back to Chief Bloodwart. "Chief, would you mind if I spoke with Mr. Lupo?"

Bloodwart smiled. "Be my guest."

Billy approached the table.

Mr. Lupo folded his arms and snarled. "I ain't talking to you, either." Then he leaned forward, looking Billy up and down. "Who are you supposed to be anyway?"

"I'm Owlboy," Billy answered. "Y'know, the superhero?"

Lupo leaned back, making a face. "Owlboy? We ain't heard hide nor hair of you for years and years. Where ya been?"

"Oh, I've been around. I was sure hoping you could help me out by describing what you saw on the street today."

The werewolf turned his head, refusing to listen. "I ain't talking," he stated.

Billy held the cockroach crunch bar in his gloved hands, wrinkling the wrapper noisily.

The werewolf slowly turned his head, his black snout twitching wetly as he sniffed the air.

"What you got there?" he asked.

"Oh, this?" Billy asked. "Just a little snack I was hoping to share with somebody who could help me out with some information." Billy paused, holding the candy bar up in front of him. "You wouldn't happen to know anybody like that, would you, Mr. Lupo?"

The werewolf licked his chops, sucking his teeth in before they could slide from his mouth again. "Is that a cockroach crunch bar?" he asked, thick, slimy drool dripping from the sides of his mouth.

"Why yes, I believe it is." Billy ran the candy under his nose and sniffed deeply.

The werewolf reached a clawed hand toward it, but Billy quickly yanked the candy away.

"Not so fast. This is only for somebody who's willing to help us here."

Mr. Lupo pulled back his hand. "It was horrible, and I'd rather not talk about it."

"That's fine." Billy tore open the wrapper. "I guess I'll just have to eat this whole cockroach crunch bar all by my lonesome."

The thought of eating the cockroach-filled candy bar was enough to make Billy hurl, but he had to convince the old werewolf he was serious.

He brought the candy bar up to his mouth, trying to ignore the spindly, chocolate-covered legs and antennas.

He was just about to take a bite, when Mr. Lupo spoke.

"I'll talk if you give me half," the old werewolf said, wiping a thick trail of spit from his mouth.

"Deal," Billy said, removing the rest of the candy bar from its wrapper. He started to hand it to the eager wolf, then yanked it back suddenly.

"Why don't you start by telling us what you remember," he said.

Mr. Lupo looked frustrated, and also sort of scared. "All right, here goes," he said, getting his courage up. "I was out for my walk, goin' to get myself a bite to eat, when I seen this van pull up in front of the Monster Central Bank."

The room was eerily quiet, except for the old werewolf's raspy breathing. "There was nothing special about the van, and I probably wouldn't've given it another look, except that the doors flew open, and these really nasty looking characters—ogres, I believe, a man and a woman—got out and headed for the bank. They nearly knocked me down trying to get to the front door."

"Ogres?" Billy asked.

"Yeah," the werewolf responded. His eyes had become glassy as he looked out across the room, remembering what he had seen. "They had bad news written all over them, and that was when I noticed that there was somebody else with 'em."

The werewolf paused, and Billy could see that he had started to shake.

"I think I might need some of that candy bar

now," the werewolf told him. "To keep up my strength and all."

Billy broke the candy bar in half and handed him the larger piece.

Mr. Lupo eagerly bit into the cockroach bar, closing his eyes as he chewed. Billy half expected his teeth to go flying, but they managed to stay in place.

"So these two ogres," Billy said to get him started again. "They had someone else with them?"

The werewolf's eyes grew wider. "Not someone—something," he stressed. "It was the most horrible creature I had ever seen, and I've seen me some pretty wild creatures in my years, let me tell you."

"Could you describe this . . . this horrible creature?" Billy asked.

Archebold immediately broke out the *Book of Creeps*, and Bugsy hunched over his sketchpad.

"Not sure if I'll be able to," Lupo said with a meaningful glance at the candy bar. "Still feeling a tad weak."

"Would the other half of the cockroach crunch bar give you the strength you need?" Billy asked.

"Y'know, it just might," the werewolf said, plucking the candy from Billy's hand and shoving the entire thing in his mouth.

"Go on, Mr. Lupo," Billy said.

The werewolf took a deep breath. "It was small, about your size," he said, pointing to Archebold. "Its skin was pink, with weird antennas that stuck out from the side of its round head, and its eyes were big and round."

Archebold flipped through the *Book of Creeps* as Bugsy's pencils flew over the drawing pad.

"It had pink, wormy fingers," Mr. Lupo went on. "Fingers that had lightning dancing from their tips."

"Lightning?" everybody inside the room said at the same time.

The werewolf nodded. "And that's not all. You shoulda seen what it did with this evil power." The old wolf paused for effect. "It reached its pink, disgusting hands out to the bank, and the bank began to shimmy and shake, and the walls came tumbling down."

Lupo stared at his own clawed hands. "It was horrible, I tell ya."

It became deathly quiet in the small room, the old werewolf's fear so thick Billy could cut it with a knife.

"I can't find anything that matches that description," Archebold said with frustration, paging through the *Book of Creeps*. "Wormy pink fingers, antennas, lightning. Nothing even remotely fits that description."

"Cause it's like nothing we've ever seen!" the werewolf wailed. "And I hope never to see it again!"

Billy glanced over at the giant spider to see if he was still drawing.

"What about you, Bugsy?" Billy asked. "Was Mr. Lupo's description good enough to give us something?"

The spider's multiple pencils were flying over the sketchpad, putting some final details on the drawing. "We've got something, all right," the spider said, holding the pad out so that only he could see. "It's terrifying," he went on, a tremble of fear in his high voice.

"Let's see it," Chief Bloodwart instructed.

Billy braced himself. If the creatures of Monstros thought it was scary, he was preparing himself for the worst. He felt Archebold's hand reach out and take hold of his arm as Bugsy turned the sketchpad around.

"It's . . . horrible," Bloodwart said, quickly looking away.

"That's it!" Mr. Lupo wailed, his dentures flying from his mouth and bouncing off the table to land on the floor. The old werewolf dove beneath the table to hide.

Billy swayed, suddenly very light-headed.

"Are you all right, sir?" Archebold asked, gripping his arm tightly.

"Yeah, I'm good," he answered. But that was far from the truth.

Bugsy's drawing was perfect, capturing every single detail Mr. Lupo had described.

In fact, the drawing of Victoria was almost as good as a photograph.

Never have I been in the presence of such raw, destructive power, Sireena Sassafras thought as she sat in the back of the van with the Victoria creature and her furry companion.

"More donuts?" she asked, holding out the box of Creepy Creams.

"Sure," Victoria said, her overly large eyes glinting with glee. "These are good."

"Don't have to ask me twice," said Mr. Flops, reaching into the box with both hands.

"I don't think I've ever seen you eat so much, Mr. Flops," Victoria said through a mouthful of jellyfish donut.

"I don't think I've ever been this hungry." The furry beast that Victoria referred to as a bunny began to eat its crystallized, cobweb-covered treat eagerly. "Matter of fact, I'm not sure I've even been hungry before. This is great!"

Sireena watched the two little strangers devour their donuts happily, glad to be keeping them in a pleasant state of mind. With the help of Victoria and Mr. Flops, she and her brother would soon be the queen and king of crime in Monstros City—as well as rich beyond their wildest dreams.

"How are we doing back there?" Sigmund called from the driver's seat. "Everybody happy?"

Sireena shifted on the many sacks of money they had just acquired from various Monstros City banks. "They're just fine. More?" Sireena asked, smiling widely, offering up more of the delectable treats.

"I'm full," Victoria said, then burped loudly.

Sireena jumped back, not sure what the sound meant.

"Good one," Flops said. The two slapped their hands together in a strange, congratulatory gesture.

"That was wicked loud," Victoria said, and started to giggle.

Nervously, Sireena joined in. "We're certainly having a good time, aren't we?"

The little creature's face suddenly grew very stern. "Hey, where are we going now?" she asked. "I thought we were going back to the cemetery."

The van took a sharp corner and Sireena tumbled from her perch atop the stack of money sacks. "Of course we're going to the shadow passage that will return you to the wondrous-sounding Bradbury that you've already told us so much about."

Sireena's brain had already filed away all the things

that the Victoria creature had told them about the world above Monstros City. It sounded absolutely fascinating, and ripe for domination. When they were through with Monstros, Bradbury would be next on the Sassafras Siblings' list of conquests. "But we have to make one more stop before—"

"We're not going to another bank, are we?" Victoria whined.

"Everything all right back there?" Sigmund called out again.

"We're good," Sireena said cheerfully. "I was just about to explain to Victoria that we need to stop at one more bank to get back the money they stole from us."

The bunny was licking cobwebs from its paws. "Can't believe that all these banks took your money and won't give it back. Didn't you call the police?"

Sireena thought quickly, the evil gears inside her criminal brain clicking away. "Ahhhhhhhhh . . . we can't go to the cops, you see," she said, lowering her voice to a whisper.

"Why?" Victoria asked. "Policemen are our friends."

The Sassafras sister shook her head. "Not here in Monstros. In fact, they work with the banks, trying to take away all the things my brother and I have worked so hard to get."

"That's awful," Mr. Flops said.

"Yeah," Victoria agreed. "It's a good thing we came along to help you."

"Exactly," Sireena said. "Without your . . . what did you call it? Your Destructo Touch? Our money would be kept from us forever."

The van came to a sudden, screeching halt and Sigmund got out.

"Humongous National Bank," he announced as he opened the van's rear doors. "Let's go show those good-for-nothing bank managers that they can't steal from the Sassafras Siblings anymore!"

"Yeah!" Victoria cried, and both she and Flops jumped out of the van.

Sireena joined them. "Well, let's go," she said, starting to cross the street. A sudden tug on her skirt stopped her and she looked down to see Victoria still on the curb, Mr. Flops by her side. "What is it?" she asked, a hint of impatience in her tone.

"I can't cross unless I hold a grown-up's hand," the pink-skinned agent of destruction said.

Sireena stared at the stubby digits wiggling for attention. She had seen what those fingers were capable of, and had no desire to touch them.

"Sigmund would love to take you across," Sireena said, grabbing hold of her brother's shoulders and spinning him toward the tiny creature.

"What am I doing?" he asked.

"You're helping me across the street," Victoria said as she reached out and took his hand.

Sireena braced herself, waiting for her brother to explode like a bubble or to burst into flames like a bonfire, but he seemed to be perfectly fine.

"Shall we go, then?" she asked, and they all bustled across the busy street to the bank entrance.

Patrons were coming and going, but all Sireena could see in her mind were dollar signs. She had a feeling that this was going to be their best haul yet.

She watched as Victoria and Flops walked toward the front door of Humongous National.

"Wait!" Sireena called out, and the others halted in their tracks. "Since this is our last bank, we need to make a special entrance, one that everybody will remember."

"Awesome," Victoria said with a hideous smile.

Sireena was truly disturbed by how ugly this creature from Bradbury was. If this was how all residents of the mysterious world above looked, she thought it must be a truly terrifying place indeed.

"Do you want me to use *it*?" Victoria asked, rubbing her tiny hands together. Standing beside her, Flops did the same.

"Oh yes," Sireena said, nodding her head slowly. "Use the Destructo Touch!"

And with a high-pitched squeal that sounded like it

might have been delight, the horrible little creature approached the front of the Humongous National Bank and laid her hands upon the building.

The wall began to shake, huge cracks appearing and snaking down to the foundation. In a matter of seconds, the front of the bank no longer existed.

"How's that?" Victoria asked, wiping the dust from her hands on the front of her pants.

"Spectacular," Sireena answered. "I couldn't have done better myself."

CHAPTER 11

"Down there!" Billy yelled, looking through the curved windshield of the Owlcopter.

A huge plume of dust had just erupted into the eerie darkness of the Monstros City sky.

"How much you wanna bet there's a bank down there?" he said, watching the thick grayish cloud drift in the sky like smoke.

Archebold aimed the sky craft toward the street.

"I'm taking us down, sir."

Victoria was running wild in the streets of Monstros City, and it appeared that her already deadly Destructo Touch had been amplified by being here.

It didn't really surprise Billy. He'd seen what this weird place did for his own strength and speed. It was only logical that Victoria's superpower—if you wanted to call it that—would be increased as well.

The Owlcopter dropped down through the thick cloud of dust, the spinning rotor blades clearing the air so that they could see.

It was just like in the other parts of the city.

Total chaos.

Monsters were running everywhere in a panic. A large, square building directly below had lost its front, the stone used to build it turned to rubble. Billy was reminded of the Constructo blocks in his garage.

"I guess I do have to go down there," he said to his friend.

Archebold flipped some switches on his control panel and a hatch slid open behind them in the floor of the copter.

"Jeez, couldn't you have fought me a little—*oh no, Billy, it's too dangerous!*—or something like that?" Billy asked.

Archebold smiled, moving the control stick around on the copter to keep it hovering in one place above the chaotic street. "You're the superhero," he said.

Billy sighed, unbuckling his seat belt and going toward the hatch. "That's what you keep telling me," he complained.

There was a spool of cable in the ceiling above the

hatch opening and Billy took hold of the end, preparing to jump.

"Are you sure there's nothing you can say to convince me not to do this?" he asked as he took the cable in his hand.

"Nope," the goblin said with a wave. "Bye-bye!"

"Thanks for thinking about it, though," Billy said as he got ready to leap down into the hatch.

"No prob" was the last thing Billy heard as he jumped, the thick cable unspooling with a whirring sound as he dropped to the street below him.

He landed in a crouch, and quickly scanned for any signs of danger. He let go of the cord, gave Archebold a wave, and the Owlcopter flew off.

Billy reached out to a passing citizen, her arms filled with grocery bags. "Excuse me."

She had one huge eye in the center of a round face. The eye bulged as she fixed him in what he thought might be a frightened stare.

"Can you tell me what's going on?" he asked her.

"It's terrible," she said, clutching her bags tighter. "One minute it was there and then it was gone. Terrible! Terrible, I tell you!"

And in a total panic, the eyeball lady ran off.

"Great," Billy muttered as he approached what used to be the front of the building. "That certainly helped."

He didn't know what to expect. All he knew was that it probably involved his five-year-old next-door neighbor, and that he had to get her out of there before she could do any more damage.

He heard voices, and moved closer to the crumbled building front. At first he heard two—a man and a woman whom he didn't recognize; at least he thought it was a man and a woman—but the third voice was unmistakable.

Victoria.

He saw the ogres first, each of them pushing carts stacked high with bags of money. Even at first glance, there was something about the two that screamed *bad guys*. Their skin was a sickly green, their heads practically square. They both had huge lower jaws and stocky, muscular bodies that reminded Billy of some gorillas he'd once seen at the zoo. The guy was dressed fairly normally in dark pants, shirt and vest, but the woman wore lots of jewelry, a flouncy blouse and a dress with flowers all over it. It looked as though she was trying to be beautiful.

Too bad she has a face that could stop a clock.

And between them both, struggling along, dragging one of the money bags with the help of a stuffed rabbit, was his five-year-old neighbor.

Stuffed rabbit?

Yep, Mr. Flops was showing more life than his own father on a football-season Sunday.

"So when we're finished here, there're only a few more banks we have to stop at. Isn't that right, Sireena?" the male ogre was saying.

"Oh yes, now that you mention it, Brother Sigmund," agreed the female beastie.

The little girl dropped her bag and crossed her arms. "I don't want to go to any more banks," she said, wearing what Billy had learned was her mad face. "I want you to take me and Mr. Flops back home."

It was all starting to make sense. Somehow these two—Sireena and Sigmund—were using Victoria to help them rob the Monstros City banks.

Yep, they were evil all right.

Billy cleared his throat.

"I'll take you home, Victoria," he said, lowering the tone of his voice to sound more superheroic.

The angry look on Victoria's face turned to one of surprise.

"Billy Hooten!" she shrieked happily. "What are you doin' here?"

"I've come to bring you home," he said, raising his hand and gesturing for her to join him.

"You look cool in that costume, Billy," she said, starting toward him.

Sireena grabbed her by the shoulder. "Are you sure you want to do that, dear?"

"Think about it," Sigmund added. His dark, shifty eyes looked at Billy with intense hatred. "Isn't this the same person who made fun of you . . . and made you cry?"

"You got that right," Mr. Flops piped up. "He was pretty mean."

Victoria stopped. The mad face was back, and she seemed to be remembering how angry she was at Billy. She put her hands on her hips. "Yeah, you were mean, Billy Hooten, and I don't think I want to be your friend anymore."

Billy rolled his eyes. Every time the little girl got mad at him, she wasn't going to be his friend anymore. *A real freakin' tragedy*, he thought disgustedly.

"Knock it off, Victoria, and c'mon," he said, holding out his gloved hand. "I gotta get you home before anybody notices you're gone and—"

"Don't listen to him," Sigmund said, moving in close and putting his hands on Victoria's shoulders. "He just wants to make you cry some more."

"Yes," Sireena agreed. "Look at him in his superhero costume, thinking he's some sort of big shot, pushing you around."

"Yeah," Victoria agreed, the mad face getting even madder. "Stupid Billy Hooten."

"Cut the crap, you two!" Billy yelled at the ogres. "Victoria is coming with me right now or she's going to get into a lot of trouble."

At first, Billy wasn't sure what happened. One second he was standing there, the next he was flying through the air. And then he realized that in a fit of anger Victoria had stomped her sneakered foot upon the ground, creating a miniearthquake that shook the streets of Monstros City.

"Don't you yell at my new bestest friends, you great big stupid-head!" she screamed.

Billy landed hard on his butt, a shock wave of pain shooting up his back and making his eyes water. The ground continued to shake, rattle and roll, and the screams of the citizenry filled the air.

He struggled to his feet, pinwheeling his arms in an attempt to keep his balance on the violently vibrating street. Quickly, he scanned the area, searching for the little girl, and gasped when he saw her teetering on the edge of a great, jagged rip in the pavement.

Billy jumped into action, springing through the air to grab Victoria and her bunny friend just when it looked as though they were about to fall into the yawning abyss. He felt his heart racing a million miles a minute as he set the little girl and her stuffed rabbit down.

"Are you all right?" he asked.

At first she was still wearing the mad face, and he thought he might be about to witness another example of the fearsome power of the Destructo Touch. But a smile broke out on Victoria's cute face as she threw her arms around his neck.

"I'm fine, thanks to you." Her hug nearly choked him. "My hero!"

"So does this mean you're not mad at me anymore?" Billy asked, peeling her arms from around his neck.

"How could I stay mad at you?" she beamed. "You're so cute."

"He *is* adorable," Flops said, pulling a donut out of a pocket hidden in his fur and taking a big bite.

Victoria looked away suddenly, her big brown eyes darting around the rubble-strewn street.

"Hey, where did my new bestest friends Sigmund and Sireena Sassafras go?" she asked.

"Good question," Billy replied, suddenly on alert. "You two stay here," he told Victoria and Flops. "I'm going to go look for them."

"Tell 'em I don't want to go to any more banks," Victoria said before snatching what was left of the donuts away from the bunny.

"Hey!" Flops screamed.

Billy could hear the little girl and the rabbit arguing

as he left them. *Good*, he thought. Maybe it would keep them out of trouble for awhile.

He was sort of hoping that Sigmund and Sireena had flown the coop. He would have liked nothing better than to get Victoria home, and then head for the garage to see what his mother had gotten for him. *Your Halloween costume problems are solved*, he heard her say inside his head, distracting him for only a moment.

But a moment was all true evil needed to strike.

Billy heard the sound of the attack before he had a chance to react. It was a strange sound, like a spitball being shot from a straw—only much louder—and he found himself wrapped in a net with heavy weights attached to the corners. He was trapped.

"And if I remember correctly, you made fun of me for investing in the Net-O-Matic," Sigmund said, coming out from behind a vehicle that had been overturned by Victoria's temper-tantrum earthquake. He was cradling a large, awkward-looking weapon in his arms. NET-O-MATIC was written in scarlet letters across its boxy shape.

Sireena skulked closer to her brother, an oversized purse slung over her shoulder. "I did no such thing," she hissed. "I'm sure I was making fun of you for something entirely different, like your ridiculous fashion sense or your aversion to bathing regularly."

"I could've sworn it was over the Net-O-Matic," Sigmund said. "But I guess you could be right."

They stood over Billy as he struggled inside the net.

"Of course I'm right," Sireena barked. She had started to fish through her large shoulder bag. "Now where did I put that disintegration ray?"

Sigmund began to laugh. "Can you believe this, sister?" he asked Sireena, who was still looking for her disintegrator gun. "Finally, a chance to destroy the one that has brought so much shame to the Sassafras name."

"I know it's in here somewhere," Sireena muttered. An entire roast chicken fell from the bag as she continued to paw through its contents.

Isn't it just like a villain to gloat over the captured hero? Billy thought as he searched the pouches of his utility belt for something to cut through the net.

"Ah, here it is," Sireena said, pulling the funky-looking weapon from inside her enormous bag. At the same time, Billy found the Monstros City equivalent of a Swiss Army knife: a spoon, a toothpick, a magnifying glass, a shoehorn, a duck-call and a corkscrew, but nothing he could use to cut his way free.

"Look at him," Sireena said, her disgustingly large lips glistening with what looked to be a fresh coat of lipstick. "Trapped as our poor mother has been trapped after suffering at his hands—at the hands of Owlboy. For one hundred years she has been locked away, her children denied her motherly affections."

Billy finally located the knife blade and opened it with a squeal of delight. It didn't look all that sharp, but beggars couldn't be choosers, and he immediately started sawing at the netting.

Sigmund had started crying, pulling a large handkerchief from his inside vest pocket and dabbing at his leaking eyes. "I miss Mom so much," he moaned.

"There, there, brother," Sireena said as she aimed her weapon. "Take comfort knowing that the one who is responsible for breaking up our happy family will soon be no more than ash, and that we'll then be free to establish ourselves as the most powerful crime family in all of Monstros City."

Sigmund smiled. "That *does* make me feel better, sister," he said.

"I knew it would." Sireena's finger tensed on the trigger of the disintegrator gun.

Billy was sawing like a maniac, but things weren't looking too good for him.

"Any last words before your ashy remains are blowing away on a gentle breeze, Owlboy?" Sireena asked with a gurgling chuckle.

"Yeah, could you give me another couple of minutes?" Billy asked, sawing furiously.

"No," Sireena spat, and prepared to fire her weapon at him.

Billy squeezed his eyes shut and waited for the pain to start. He wasn't sure how being hit by a disintegrator ray would feel, but he imagined it would hurt like heck.

A familiar hiccup suddenly shot through the ground, and the earth erupted in a powerful geyser of water that lifted the Sassafras Siblings into the air.

"See, I can help you, Billy," a familiar voice announced proudly as the net fell apart and he was free.

Victoria stood there with Mr. Flops, a big smile on her face.

"You saved me?" Billy asked, amazed.

"Well, I couldn't let her shoot you," the little girl said. "Then who would be my bestest friend?"

She put her arms around his waist and gave him another big hug. "I think I'm going to marry you when I get big."

Billy shuddered. Then a breeze began to blow, and he looked up to see the Owlcopter descending. He waved as the bright yellow craft landed and Archebold scrambled from the cockpit.

"I would've been here sooner but I couldn't find a decent parking space," the goblin complained.

"No problem," Billy said.

Victoria still had her arms around him. Archebold gave her a look, and then gave Billy the eye.

"This is Victoria," Billy explained. "My next-door neighbor. She's got the Destructo Touch."

The goblin jumped back as if afraid.

"Don't worry," Billy explained. "She's perfectly harmless when she's not listening to the Sassafras Siblings." He hooked a finger behind him at the spewing waterspout. "I suggest we slip the Owlcuffs on those two and get them over to police headquarters—"

"Sassafras Siblings?" Archebold asked. "What Sassafras Siblings?"

Billy turned around to look up at the top of the waterspout. "They might be hard to see, they're right up . . . wait a minute."

The Sassafras Siblings were gone.

"They were there a minute ago," Billy said. He looked down at Mr. Flops, who was eating another donut. "Did you see where they went?"

The stuffed rabbit pointed down the street.

"Great," Billy said with disappointment.

The Sassafrasses had gotten away.

"Look at me!" Sireena wailed, standing knee-deep in the putrid water flowing within the tunnel of Monstros

City's underground sewage system. "I'm a filthy, disgusting mess!"

Sigmund sloshed through the fetid waters ahead of her. "Come on before they get the bright idea to look for us down here," he snapped.

"I . . . I'm not sure I want to be a criminal mastermind anymore," Sireena's voice echoed up to him from the tunnel, stopping him dead in his tracks.

Sigmund spun around. "What did you say?" he asked incredulously.

His sister was crying, her large hands plastered to her face. Her makeup ran from her skin in rivulets, making it look as though she were melting.

"I don't know how much more disappointment I can take," she sobbed.

Sigmund splashed through the raw sewage to stand beside her.

"Is that any way for a Sassafras to talk?" he asked. "Where would our most beautiful Mother Sassafras be if she had shared your defeatist attitude?"

Sireena looked up, her face streaked with color. "Not in prison?" she answered.

"Exactly!" Sigmund bellowed. "No, wait a minute, that didn't turn out the way I wanted it to," he said.

"Perhaps it's time we hang it up," Sireena suggested. "Maybe we need to be the first generation to admit that we can't defeat Owlboy."

Sigmund couldn't believe what his sister was saying. The shocking power of her words seemed to freeze his vocal cords.

"Maybe it's time we leave this life of crime and do something rewarding with our lives?" she continued.

Sigmund felt his fingers twist into claws as he reached for the tree-trunk thickness of his sister's neck.

"Kittens!" she suddenly squealed.

He jumped back, startled. "Kittens?"

Sireena nodded. "You like kittens, right?"

"Between two slices of bread," he scowled.

"How nice would it be to raise cute little kittens, and give them away to all the little children of Monstros City."

She went on and on about kittens and flowers and other topics too terrifying for words, and Sigmund's eyes desperately darted about for something, anything that he could use to get her to snap out of it.

His gaze landed on the DANGER sign that covered a large clump of multicolored wires on the tunnel wall, and his heart fluttered with joy. Diving across the sewer water, he took hold of the colored wires and gave them a ferocious yank, tearing them from the wall, and plunged the sizzling ends into the water.

There was a searing explosion of white light, and the sensation that he was flying, before the sudden pain of impact as his body hit the tunnel wall. Sigmund slid down the curved, cold stone onto the ledge.

Violently he shook his head, attempting to clear away the fog, and looked to see the water glowing with an eerie light as electricity from the wires flowed through it.

"Sireena," he gasped, scrambling along the ledge. Careful not to fall into the electrically charged water, he searched for a shut-off switch on the tunnel wall.

He found what he was looking for, pushing the switch up and cutting the power to the wires. The water immediately stopped bubbling and glowing and gradually became very still.

There was no sign of his sister.

"Sireena," he called out again, jumping off the ledge into the water. His hands fished around beneath the water, searching for his sibling.

What have I done? Sigmund panicked. Had the voltage been so high that he'd boiled her away to nothing?

What would he tell his mother?

The bubbling of the sewer water made him turn around in time to catch sight of his sister slowly rising from the filthy depths. Sigmund was overjoyed, but also feared for his life.

"You weren't in your right mind," he began to explain. "I had to do something before—"

"No need to apologize, brother dear," Sireena said, small crackling bolts of electricity dancing across the surface of her large teeth. "You did the right thing."

Sigmund recoiled. "I did?"

His sister slowly nodded. "Oh yes indeed. And in doing so, you've stimulated my thoughts to go in the most interesting of directions."

"I did?" Sigmund repeated.

"I know where we must go if we are to achieve our hopes and desires," Sireena said dreamily, sparks jumping from one earring-decorated lobe to the other. "The child with the Destructo Touch, she provided us with the answer to our predicament, but we did not yet understand."

Sigmund really had no clue what his sister was talking about and began to wonder if the electric shock had loosened all her screws.

"I still don't know what—"

"She was from the world above," Sireena whispered.

"The world above?"

She nodded slowly. "A world without Owlboy."

And then it hit him. "A world without anybody to stop us." A sly smile slithered across his face.

"A world ripe for the picking," Sireena said.

Sigmund at last understood.

Ripe for the picking indeed.

Archebold and Halifax entered the Snack Room wearing heavily padded protective suits that made them look like walking pot holders.

"What are you dressed like that for?" Billy asked from the table where he sat with Victoria and Mr. Flops. They were enjoying some of Monstros' special treats: Bloodberry Pie, fried lizard lips, cockroach custard and three heaping mugs of poltergeist potion.

"Can't be too careful with her in here," Halifax said, pointing to Victoria with a heavily padded finger.

"Yeah," Archebold agreed. "Never know when she might decide to unleash the full force of her destructive power."

The little girl was laughing hysterically as a mug of poltergeist potion danced around in front of her. Mr. Flops was eating like crazy, grabbing handfuls of fried lizard lips and shoving them into his mouth.

"Yeah, she certainly does seem to be a threat," Billy said sarcastically.

"Not now," Archebold said. "But you saw what she did out there to the city."

Halifax nodded, his eyes peeking out from behind the visor of his protective headgear. It amazed Billy how scared they seemed to be of the five-year-old.

"I was only helping my new friends get their money back from the mean bank people," Victoria explained as she dug into an oozing piece of Bloodberry Pie.

"Yeah, it wasn't as if she did all that damage on purpose. She was tricked," Billy said, coming to Victoria's defense.

"We both were," Flops said, and belched loudly, a tuft of white stuffing flying from his mouth. "Excuse me."

"The Sassafras Siblings are extremely tricky," Archebold agreed. "That family has been a thorn in the side of Monstros City law enforcement for what seems like forever. The last Owlboy defeated their father, which resulted in him being trapped in Dimension X, and Mother Sassafras got sent away not too long before he disappeared all those years ago. The Siblings have been on the loose since. As a matter of fact, it wouldn't surprise me in the least if they were responsible for the robberies involving the Sludge Sloggers," Archebold added.

"Ya think?" Billy asked.

"Getting some less than intelligent life-form to do their dirty work," Archebold explained, making a point to look at Victoria. "I think it's got their filthy fingerprints all over it."

It makes sense, Billy thought as he stroked his chin. And it just proved all the more how dangerous the Sassafras Siblings were, and how they needed to be caught and brought to justice.

"If only I hadn't screwed up," Billy moaned, "they'd be in jail right now instead of on the loose."

"We'll get them," Halifax said. "Evil has a real hard time staying out of trouble, especially in Monstros."

"Yeah, they'll be in custody in no time. But first Halifax and I have to help repair some of the damage done by your little friend here," Archebold explained. "And you have to get her out of the city pronto."

"Was the mayor mad?" Billy asked.

The goblin had had a long conversation with Mayor Grumbleguts when things had calmed down a bit on the streets.

"Let's just say she won't be getting an invitation to the gargoyle gala at the end of the month, if you know what I mean," Archebold said.

Billy nodded, understanding exactly. The mayor was as afraid of what Victoria might still do as Archebold and Halifax were. Thinking about the destruction he'd seen on the streets of Monstros, he really couldn't blame them.

"I better think about getting her back then," Billy said, turning in his seat to see that the little girl had fallen fast asleep, her pigtailed head resting on her hands.

"I think she's pooped," Flops commented, grabbing Victoria's plate, which contained what was left of her Bloodberry Pie, and sliding it over in front of him.

"Don't you ever get full?" Billy asked.

"I'll let you know if it happens," the stuffed rabbit said, shoving forkfuls of the dripping red pie into his hungry maw.

Billy pushed his chair back and carefully approached the sleeping child. "Hey, Victoria," he whispered. He reached out and tapped her on the shoulder.

Both Halifax and Archebold gasped as one. "Careful," Archebold warned.

"Calm down, guys," Billy scolded.

"Is it time to get up, Ma?" Victoria said, yawning loudly as she looked around the Snack Room with bleary eyes.

"It's time to go home," Billy said as he took her hand and helped her down from the chair.

"Time to go home?" she slurred, smacking her lips.

"Yep," Billy said, pushing her chair in beneath the table.

"Is Flops coming?" she asked as Billy led her toward the door.

"If he can stop stuffing his face, I'm sure he'll be coming," Billy answered, turning to give Mr. Flops a look of disgust.

The stuffed rabbit had finished all the pie and was now eating the crumbs remaining on the lizard lips plate.

"I'm comin', I'm comin'," the rabbit said as he hopped down from his seat and walked across the room to join them.

Billy pressed a circular red button on the wall and the door slid open with a snaky hiss.

"I'll get these two home and be back to deal with the Sassafras problem as soon as I can," Billy told his friends, who were standing clumped together across the room.

"Gotcha, boss," Halifax said.

"Hurry back," Archebold added with a wave.

Victoria, seeming more awake now, turned around to face the pair. "See ya later, guys," she said.

Her sudden movement caused the goblin and the troll to jump back. Halifax tripped over the snack cart and crashed to the floor. Archebold went to his aid, helping him up.

"Catch ya later, fellas," Billy said with a roll of his eyes, and he, Victoria and Flops left the Snack Room and headed down one of the long, winding hallways of the Roost on their way to the shadow passage that would lead them home.

"Which way do we go?" Victoria asked sleepily as they stood in the deep darkness, multiple roads leading off in many different directions.

Billy closed his eyes, feeling the pull of the correct path. "This one," he said, holding Victoria's hand as they continued on their way.

"What a day . . . or is it night?" Flops said as he followed them. "Who can tell in these parts?"

"Yeah, it does get sort of confusing," Billy said. "It's always nighttime in Monstros City."

"I hope Mom isn't mad," Victoria said. "I've been away from the house for an awful long time."

"Don't worry too much," Billy explained as they walked down the curving, dark tunnel. "Time works sort of funny in Monstros."

"Funny how?" Victoria asked.

"Well, when we get back, hardly any time will have passed at all. Isn't that weird?"

"That's crazy stuff," Flops chimed in. "Any other weirdo differences between where we're going and bizarro city?"

Billy knew one major difference for the stuffed rabbit, and felt bad that he had to tell him.

"Yeah, you won't be alive anymore up above," Billy said. "Sorry."

Flops stopped walking.

They continued on for a bit, and were all very quiet, until Victoria broke the silence.

"You could always stay here, Mr. Flops, so that you could be alive. I wouldn't be too sad," the little girl said. But her voice was shaking.

Great, Billy thought. All he needed was for her to start crying again, but Mr. Flops handled the situation just fine.

"That's mighty nice of you, Vic, but I think I'd rather stay with you whether I'm alive or not."

Victoria snatched the rabbit up in her arms for a big hug. "That's what I hoped you would say," she said, tossing the bunny over her shoulder to carry him.

It wasn't much longer before they reached the open area, which contained the stairs that would bring them up into the Sprylock family mausoleum and home.

"Almost there," Billy said as he looked down at the little girl. She could barely keep her eyes open. Flops had fallen asleep against Victoria's shoulder and was snoring loudly.

"What's the matter?" Billy asked.

"I'm tired," she said, rubbing her eyes.

"Do you think you can make it up those stairs?" he asked, suspecting what her answer would be.

She shook her head no.

Billy sighed, about to ask the question that he was sure he'd regret.

"Do you want me to carry you?"

Victoria nodded happily, hopping onto his back. She wasn't heavy at all, the magic or whatever it was about Monstros City that increased his strength and agility still with him.

"All right, let's do this," he said, and started up the winding staircase.

About halfway there, Billy realized that he should probably have a talk with the girl. That would be all he needed, to have her start to spout crazy stuff about being in the mausoleum and there being a monster city beneath it, and him being a superhero called Owlboy.

With his luck, somebody might just believe it.

"Hey, Victoria, before we get home, I want to talk to you about all this stuff," he said, trudging up the stairs. He could feel the little girl getting heavier, and the muscles in his legs start to burn the farther he got from Monstros and the closer he got to the surface world.

"We should make it our own little secret, don't ya

think?" he asked. "Just between me and you, what do you think of that?"

His question was met with a piggish snore. Victoria was fast asleep, clutching her stuffed bunny, which had returned to normal, lovingly to her face.

CHAPTER 12

The square of light above gradually loomed closer, and it was a good thing. Billy thought he might have a heart attack, lugging the little girl on his back. She weighed more than he thought she did, and he had to wonder what her parents had been feeding her.

Billy poked his head up from the stone coffin, climbing up and over the side to the dusty stone floor. He laid Victoria, who was still fast asleep, down on the ground and went to retrieve his backpack so that he could change out of his costume and into his normal clothes.

He shoved his Owlboy suit back into the pack and went to wake the little girl up.

"Hey, Victoria." Billy couldn't resist wetting the end of his pinkie finger and sticking it inside her ear.

Wet willies were the ultimate way to be woken up.

Victoria's face went from calm and serene to absolutely disgusted.

"Gross!" she screamed, swatting Billy's hands away as she rubbed at her ear. "That's the nastiest thing ever, Billy Hooten!"

Billy couldn't help but laugh. "Sorry, couldn't resist."

The little girl grabbed her stuffed bunny and threw it at him. "Better be careful or I'll be mad at you again," she said.

Billy caught Mr. Flops and on reflex shoved the stuffed animal in his backpack.

"Yeah, yeah, yeah, you'll hate me forever. We gotta get you home."

Billy took this opportunity to try an experiment.

"Boy, it's sure weird that I found you in here fast asleep . . . bet you had some pretty crazy dreams."

"I didn't fall asleep in here, stupid-head," the charming child yelled. She brushed off the back of her jeans. "I went to Monstros City and used my Destructo Touch."

She made a crazy sound, holding out her hands to touch him.

"Knock it off," Billy said, swatting at one of her pigtails.

"And you rescued me from the Sassafras kids, who I

thought were my new bestest friends but were using me to rob banks instead."

Billy stood at the mausoleum door. "Sounds pretty crazy," he said. "Are you sure you didn't dream all that?"

Victoria smiled at him. "Are you trying to trick me, Billy Hooten?"

"Heaven forbid," he muttered, knowing that it was pointless to try to convince the little girl otherwise.

The two started on the path through the Pine Hill Cemetery, heading toward the wall that ran along the back of Billy's yard.

"So Monstros City and me being a superhero is going to be our superspecial secret, right?" he asked her.

She had picked up an acorn from the ground and was playing with it. "Why?"

He had to think fast. "Cause it will be just like in the comic books, where only really special people with special powers of their own know about the superhero and his secret hideout." He held his breath, waiting for her answer.

Victoria walked alongside him quietly, playing with her acorn. "And you can't tell anybody about my Destructo Touch, right?" she asked.

"I promise," he said. "We'll both have superspecial secrets."

She nodded happily, eyes twinkling.

They reached the wall and he picked her up, positive that she had to weigh at least two hundred pounds, and helped her over into his yard.

"So are you going to come back in the garage and help me finish my Halloween costume?" he asked.

Victoria went to her Big Wheel, which was still parked in front of the garage door, and plopped down on it.

"Nah, I'm bored with boy stuff," she said, and started to pedal down the driveway. "Think I'm gonna go play with my dollies."

And just like that she was on her way, the sound of the plastic bike's wheels fading off in the distance.

Billy looked at his watch and felt like he'd been punched in the stomach by Randy Kulkowski. The Halloween party for school was only hours away, and he still didn't have a costume.

Or do I? Billy thought, remembering the package his mother had left him.

He couldn't get inside the garage fast enough.

The shipping sticker on the top of the box said it was from someplace called The Masqueraders Ball in Bugsquirt, Michigan—*wherever the heck that was*.

It didn't take a rocket scientist to figure out that his

mother had ordered him a costume. Billy stood over the box, feeling the prickly sensation of nervous perspiration breaking out on his back and neck. One part of him wanted to rip the package open to reveal what was inside, while another just wanted to back away really slowly.

But time was running out. With the contest only hours away, Billy really didn't have much of a choice. It was either wrack his brains to the point of them exploding and running out his ears to come up with a costume, and then making it, or opening up the box and seeing what his mother had gotten for him.

How bad can it be? he thought with a nervous chuckle, sliding his fingers beneath the brown packing paper and ripping it from the box.

Here it was, the moment of truth. Billy stuck his fingernail through the packing tape that sealed the box closed and tore it open.

As long as it's not a monkey in a tutu, he thought with a nervous laugh as he reached into the box. *Who knows, maybe it'll be something really cool*, he mused, trying to think of something his mother might've stumbled across somewhere that she'd thought would be appropriate for winning the contest.

But no matter how hard he tried, his brain remained blank, which made the level of anticipation and dread he was currently facing all the worse.

He took a deep breath and pulled the wrapped package from inside the box in a flurry of Styrofoam packing.

At first he had no idea what he was looking at. The costume was white, but it also had black spots. He turned the package over in his hands and still couldn't figure out what it was supposed to be.

He reached down into the box, through the layer of packing peanuts, and found what he was looking for.

The receipt. His eyes darted across the paper until he found the name of the costume. *Crazy Cow. With Real Working Udders!*

"A cow!" he screamed, tossing the costume back in the box. "She expects me to win the hundred-dollar gift certificate as a stupid cow!"

Billy was on the verge of losing it. As far as he could remember, a cow—or any other farm animal costume—had never won the Connery Elementary School Costume Extravaganza.

"Deep breaths, Hooten," he said, feeling himself becoming a bit light-headed. This was awful, terrible even. What was he going to do?

He thought about running around in a circle and screaming like a nut, but knew that wouldn't do him much good.

It was sort of funny: here he was, a superhero who had done battle with Slovakian Rot-toothed Hopping

Monkey Demons, Sludge Sloggers and bank-robbing squids, and not having the right costume for a Halloween contest was going to kick his butt.

When he looked at it that way, it all kinda seemed stupid.

But he still really wanted to win that gift certificate.

Coming to the slow realization that things weren't looking too good for him, Billy picked up the cow costume *with real working udders* and tore open the packaging.

He held the black and white outfit before him, disturbed by the rubber udders that stuck out from the costume's front. "There's no way I could wear this," he said with disgust.

But then he remembered his mother, and how proud of herself she had looked when she'd brought the package into the garage. She really believed that she had gotten him something special.

Billy didn't want to hurt her feelings, but there was no way he was going to show up at the Costume Extravaganza dressed in this unless . . .

He could feel the beginning of an idea forming inside his head. Billy looked around the garage at the various odds and ends that he had found in people's trash over the years and used on his various secret projects: rubber tubing, bubble wrap, an old-fashioned hair dryer, electric curlers. It was a veritable treasure trove of stuff that he always believed would come in handy someday.

And perhaps today was that day.

He looked at the cow suit again, his imagination in overdrive. He wouldn't even dream of being just a cow for Halloween, but what if he took it to another level. What if this wasn't a normal cow?

The cogs were spinning inside his brain.

What if this was a cow exposed to massive amounts of cosmic radiation that had leaked from the propulsion reactors of a crashed spacecraft? he wondered.

Billy felt a wicked smile spread across his face as he looked at the cow costume in a whole new light.

He had a lot of work to do.

Victoria should have been asleep hours ago.

When she had first come home, she had been certain that she was going to get in trouble for being away for so long, but found that her mommy and daddy hadn't seemed to notice that she'd been gone.

At first she thought it was all kinda confusing, and even asked her mom, who was sitting at the kitchen table reading one of her magazines, if she had missed her. Her mommy had looked up for a second, smiled, patted her on the head like she always did when she didn't want to be bothered and told her to go play.

Maybe I wasn't gone that long, Victoria thought as she headed to the basement to see if Daddy had missed her more than Mommy.

Daddy was watching one of his football games and didn't even look at her when she came down the stairs. She doubted that he would have even talked to her if she hadn't stood in front of his giganticle television and spread her arms so she blocked the screen.

He noticed her then, and told her to go upstairs to bother Mommy.

Leaving the downstairs playroom, Victoria had come to the conclusion that her daddy hadn't missed her either, and that Billy might've been right that lots of time might have gone by in that funny Monstros place, but not as much had gone by here.

It was all very crazy, and for a second she wished she knew how to tell time so that she could see how crazy it really was, but became distracted when Mom had called to her, asking if she wanted a juice box and some animal crackers.

She would have preferred some more poltergeist potion and fried lizard lips, but didn't think her mom had bought any the last time she was shopping at Big Frank's Shop & Save. Victoria had made a mental note to find the lizard lips section the next time she went shopping with her.

Fried lizard lips are awesome!

She spent the rest of the day staying out of Daddy's hair and making some Halloween decorations that she and her mom hung on the front and back doors. Before she knew it, suppertime had come and gone and it was time for her to go to bed.

Victoria didn't think the day would ever come to an end. It felt as though it had lasted twenty-gazillion hours.

Not having any problems with bedtime, she'd gone up to her room, washed up and changed into her Barbie pajamas. It didn't take more than a couple seconds to realize that she really wasn't very tired, and she decided that it might be cool to have a tea party with her dollies.

She'd been tea-partying for a bit when she started to feel her eyes getting heavy, and she knew it wouldn't be long before she fell asleep.

"Guess we're gonna hafta wrap this up, girls," she told her dolls. "I'm gettin' a little sleepy."

And it was then that she noticed the sound of a car door shutting outside. Victoria got up from the party and went to the window, looking down into Billy's driveway. She'd arrived in time to see Mr. Hooten getting in the car, with Billy right behind him. He was holding a great big box under his arm, and she figured it was his Halloween costume.

Watching the car drive away, she wondered what Billy had decided to be. She hoped that her suggestion of a fairy princess was the one he'd gone with.

Billy would be an awesome-looking fairy princess.

Unable to fight back a mighty yawn, Victoria decided it was time to go to sleep and left the window to climb into her bed. She was just about to squirm beneath the covers when it hit her.

"Where are you, Mr. Flops?" she asked, scrambling down from her bed to look around her room. "This isn't one bit funny," she said, looking through her toy box and then her closet for the bunny rabbit.

But she couldn't find him, and she was just about to start crying when she remembered the last time she had seen him.

He hadn't been alive anymore, and she had thrown him at Billy after he had given her a wet willie. She remembered Billy putting him inside his backpack, and the last place she had seen Billy's backpack was in his garage.

Victoria quickly got out of her pajamas, putting on her bright pink sweatsuit, a gift from her grandma Wiggins, and her sneakers.

She knew her mommy and daddy wouldn't let her go outside this late, so she had to be extra-sneaky. *What was it that Billy called her when she came outside without her parents knowing?* She tried to remember, silently coming down the stairs from her room.

Ninja Girl, that was it.

Daddy was still in the basement—she could hear him cheering for his favorite team—and Mommy was sitting in the living room looking through more of her magazines and having some of her special grape juice.

One of these days, Victoria thought, she would like to have some of that special grape juice. Mommy really seemed to love it.

Without anybody noticing, she went out the kitchen door and into the backyard. The spotlights in the yard went on automatically, and she crossed over into Billy's driveway on her way to the garage.

But then she heard voices—familiar ones—and ducked down behind some trash barrels, peaking out carefully so she wouldn't be seen.

"Help me, you imbecile!" Sireena Sassafras said to her brother, who had already come over from the cemetery and was standing in Billy's yard. Sireena was on top of the wall, her giant pocketbook slung over her shoulder. Sigmund leaned a really big-looking gun against the wall, and put out his hands.

"Jump down and I'll catch you," he said to her.

"You'd like that, wouldn't you," Victoria heard Sireena say. "For me to trust you completely with my safety. But of course I have no choice: I either trust you, or miss out on our hunt for Owlboy."

Hunt for Owlboy? That doesn't sound very nice, Victoria thought.

"Catch me!" Sireena said, jumping down into her brother's waiting arms. But Sigmund stumbled backward, and the two fell onto the grass in a squealing pile.

They sounded like the piggies at the farm she and her parents had visited a few weeks ago, and she clamped a hand over her mouth so they wouldn't hear her laughing.

Finally they picked themselves up from the ground.

"How did I know you'd disappoint me again?" Sireena said, brushing leaves and grass from her big behind.

Sigmund stomped away from his sister to get his gun. "I won't disappoint where it counts the most," he said.

Sireena went to the wall and pulled her own really big gun down from where she had left it. "Something tells me you'll fail at that as well," she said.

"I'll make you eat those words," he snarled at her, and the monster walked away from his sister standing in the center of the yard. Victoria wasn't sure what he was doing, but he looked like he was sniffing the air. And as he sniffed, he moved his big fat head slowly around.

"There!" he said, suddenly stopping. "I have his stink."

Sireena came to stand beside him, her big monster eyes looking huge in the darkness.

"Are you sure?" she asked.

"Positive," Sigmund answered with a creepy smile. "Let's go get him."

And the two monsters ran off, staying close to the shadows as they headed in the direction of Billy's school.

"Oh my goodness," Victoria squeaked, popping up from behind the barrel. She ran to the garage and tried the doorknob.

Locked.

But she remembered where she'd seen Billy find the key. Victoria ran back to the barrel, and using her five-year-old strength, dragged it over to the door to stand on so that she could reach the key that was hidden above the doorframe.

"Gotcha!" she said as her fingers found it, hopping down from the barrel and unlocking the door.

"Mr. Flops!" she said excitedly as she turned on the garage lights. "We need to help Billy right away before those nasty Sassafrasses try to get him."

She found Billy's backpack with Mr. Flops sticking out from the top. As she plucked her bunny from the bag, her eyes caught sight of what else her bestest friend's bag had inside it.

His costume.

"This looks like a job for Owlboy, Mr. Flops," Victoria said as she picked up the bag and ran from the garage.

Running as fast as she could, she crossed the driveway into her own yard and found her Big Wheel.

"Hopefully we won't be too late," she said, putting Billy's backpack on and shoving Mr. Flops down between her legs.

"Hold onto your carrots, I'm gonna be going wicked fast," Victoria said as she started to pedal the Big Wheel as fast as she could.

She must've been going a bazillion miles an hour.

CHAPTER 13

The excitement backstage at the Connery Elementary School Costume Extravaganza was so thick it could be cut with a lightsaber.

The kids from first, second and third grades were out on stage for their halloween pageant, dressed as ghosts, pumpkins, witches and spiders. Billy could hear them singing a song about a lonely pumpkin and rolled his eyes. He remembered doing the exact same song a few years ago when he was little.

His friends were running around like maniacs and hadn't noticed his arrival, costume box tucked under his arm. He was still a bit angry at them, but at least now he had a costume.

Oh boy, did he.

"By the prickling in my thumbs, something wicked this way comes!" said a squeaky voice. Billy turned to see Kathy B in one of the best witch costumes he'd ever seen.

"Hey, Billy," she said. "Whaddya think?" She spun around so he could see the whole costume, which was made up of tattered black and gray strips of cloth. Her face was painted a sickly green, and she had an awesome fake crooked nose. Her hair was wild and crazy, and Billy half expected bats to come flying out of it.

"Nice," he said simply.

"I'm Witch Number One, Act 1, scene three of *Macbeth*," she said proudly. "Pretty cool, eh?"

"Yep," Billy agreed.

"What's in the box?" she asked, pointing a clawed finger.

He was about to answer when the Grim Reaper showed up.

Billy had to admit that it too was a pretty awesome costume, made in such a way that whoever was underneath the long black robes and hood appeared at least seven feet tall. The eyes on the white skull face within the darkness of the hood glowed a creepy red as the reaper raised a very realistic-looking scythe.

"So should they just give me first prize now?" asked a

muffled voice, and Dwight's sweaty face popped out from somewhere in the belly of the death costume. He smiled his cooler than ice smile. "Bet you've never seen a costume this awesome before. C'mon, admit it, Hooten. This one's a killer."

"It's good," Billy agreed noncommittally, clutching the box containing the mutated cow costume all the tighter. He was beginning to think that his improvisation might not be enough to win.

"I bet the *real* Grim Reaper doesn't look this good," Dwight said with a sly smile and a wink. "Is that your costume there?" he asked, reaching out with his plastic scythe to tap on the box.

"Don't put that thing anywhere near me," Danny Ashwell announced as he came around the corner, wearing what appeared to be a green trash bag. His arms and legs were sticking out from the side, his face was painted the same color as the plastic bag and he was wearing a green shower cap. "You'll tear through my elastic membrane and release my cytoplasm."

"What the heck are you supposed to be?" Dwight asked with a sneer.

"I'm a paramecium," Danny answered with an eye roll. "I thought it would be freakin' obvious."

Everybody just stared, their mouths hanging open.

"Here's my pellicle membrane," he explained,

touching the crinkly surface of his trash bag–covered body. "And my cilia," he added, waving his arms around and spinning in a circle. "Inside, of course, you can imagine the cytoplasm, the trichocysts, the gullet, the macronucleus and the micronucleus."

The staring continued.

"Didn't anybody pay attention in Mr. DeVirgillio's biology class?" he asked.

"So, you're, like, a bug?" Dwight asked, scratching his nose with the tip of the scythe.

Danny buried his face in his hands, and for a moment, Billy felt that his costume wasn't going to be the worst one after all.

"Pssst! Pssssssssssst!" Somebody hiding behind the stacked boxes of Christmas pageant props hissed.

"Who's that?" Kathy B asked.

"Oh yeah," Danny said. "Reggie wants me to announce him." From the sleeve of his cilia, Danny pulled out a wrinkled piece of paper, unfolded it and began to read.

" 'From the darkest reaches of space he has come, hiding in plain sight amongst normal household appliances. He is our only hope against the invading forces of the Metamorphobots. He is . . .' "

Danny paused as Reggie emerged from hiding.

"Reggie the Transmogrifier!"

With great difficulty, Reggie shambled over to them. The costume was obviously handmade, but really interesting. It looked as if it was made almost entirely out of paper towel and toilet paper rolls that had been painted blue.

From within his helmet, made from a spray-painted cardboard box, Reggie smiled, displaying the only real metal on the entire robot costume. His elaborate braces shone brightly, and Billy had to wonder if his friend had found some way to polish them.

"Do you guys know how long I've been working on this?" Reggie asked as one of his rolls fell off his costume and hit the floor. "Could you get that for me, Bill?"

Billy picked up the bright blue paper towel roll and handed it to his friend.

"Thanks," Reggie said, attempting to reattach it. "The glue must not've been dry enough."

"Wow, ain't we all a sight?" Kathy B said, and Billy felt everyone's eyes on him. "So, Bill," she continued, "what've you come up with this year?"

"Still think you've got a chance of winning?" Dwight asked, his head disappearing into the belly of his Grim Reaper costume.

"It would have to be mighty special to beat this group," Reggie said, another one of his paper rolls falling to the floor.

"He might not have anything, but remember, we still got Randy and Mitchell to deal with," Danny reminded them, and they all got very quiet.

But Billy didn't mind, because it distracted them from him.

"Who knows what those two have come up with," Billy said.

"So, you got something that could beat them, Billy?" Reggie asked. Another blue tube dropped off his body.

"Yeah, Bill," Kathy B added. "Let's see what you've come up with this year."

"Just hope it's got nothing to do with biology," Danny said sadly.

"Let's see it, Hooten," Dwight demanded in his scariest Grim Reaper voice.

Billy was about to give the story of his mutated cow costume when a swarm of ghosts, witches, spiders and pumpkins flooded into the backstage area, squealing and laughing.

From the stage, they could hear Mrs. McKinney's voice announcing that it was time for the costume competition.

"That's us!" Dwight cried, moving toward the stage, Billy's costume already forgotten.

All the others followed except for Kathy B. "So are you gonna be in the contest?"

"Yeah," Billy answered. "But can you do me a favor?"

"Sure, what do ya need?"

Billy set the box down and opened it. "Could you ask Mrs. McKinney to read my name last so I can get ready?"

"Sure thing, Billy," Kathy B said, darting toward the curtain to wait with the others.

This is it, Billy thought, finding a nice dark corner backstage to get into his costume. *May the best man—or girl—win.* He pulled the costume from the box, being extra-careful not to squirt his udders.

He finished putting his costume on, sealed up the front with Velcro snaps and then went to the restroom at the far end of the backstage area to take a look at himself in the mirror that hung from the back of the door. "Dear God," Billy cried, staring at his reflection. "I'm an abomination." He was the strangest cow he had ever seen, but still a cow. The tips of the udders protruding from the costume's belly had started to leak a nasty-looking green substance.

Good that isn't the real thing, Billy thought, grabbing some paper towels to clean up the mess. The actual corrosive substance that he imagined leaking from the udders would have eaten through the floor, and probably the earth.

"Mitchell Spivey and Randal Kulkowski," he heard

Mrs. McKinney read and he was on the move, running around the young ghosts, witches, pumpkins and spiders that were still hyped up on candy corn and whatever other kinds of sugary treats they could shove into their mouths.

"What is that?" a spider kid asked as he ambled past.

"Think it's some kind of cow," answered a ghost.

"He's leakin'," said a witch.

"Ewwwwwwwwwwwwwww!" they all groaned.

If he'd had the time, he would have squirted them with his udders of doom, but he had to see what Randy and Mitchell had come up with.

There were still a couple more kids waiting to be called—a kid dressed as an astronaut, a winged fairy and a fireman. Billy pushed past them, excusing himself so that he could get a look. From what he could hear, Randy and Mitchell were getting quite the reaction.

Stepping to the side of the fairy, Billy looked out onto the stage and gasped.

The costume was amazing. It made him feel sick to his stomach and jealous at the same time.

From what he could figure of the design, both Randy and Mitchell were inside the bulky green body of the suit, one likely sitting on the shoulders of the other. The costume had a great big square-shaped head and long, apelike arms with tufts of fake hair glued all over them.

Billy watched as the Mitchell/Randy beast stomped around the stage and the audience applauded wildly.

The monster turned toward him and Billy got a good look at the giant-sized head and its great, bulging, bloodshot eyes, which looked to be made from papier-mâché. Its enormous mouth was on a sort of hinge, and as it opened and closed Billy could see the grinning face of Randy peeking out from inside.

Looking at the monster costume head-on, and ignoring Randy's ugly mug, Billy had the odd sense that he had seen this beastie, or at least something like it, before.

And then it hit him.

It had a striking resemblance to a Sassafras Sibling.

Keeping close to the shadows around the brick structure, the Sassafras Siblings watched the trail of pink-skinned humans entering the school building.

"What should we call them?" Sigmund asked his sister.

Sireena was desperately trying to look at her reflection in a handheld mirror. She couldn't look a mess before destroying her archenemy and conquering his home world.

"Who?" she asked her brother as she smacked her enormous lips, making sure her lipstick was evenly applied.

"Them." He pointed. "The humans."

Satisfied, Sireena put her mirror away. "You already answered the question, idiot. They're humans."

"But don't you think that's sort of boring? I think we should rename them, especially if we're going to conquer them and all."

Sireena checked her rifle again to be certain it was loaded. It was, and she felt a thrill of excitement pass through her as she thought about it turning the enemy to dust.

"I imagine you've already thought of a new name," she said to her brother.

"Pinkies," Sigmund said with an enormous smile that showed off multiple rows of crooked teeth.

He has Father's smile, Sireena thought as she stared at him, suppressing the urge to knock all his teeth out. She had never really liked Father.

"Pinkies?" she asked, her face twisted up as if she'd smelled something really bad. "I don't like it."

"Of course you like it," Sigmund barked. "It's perfect. They're all soft and pink . . . and . . . and soft . . . and pink. It's perfect and you know it!"

Sireena rolled her eyes. "When I have the

opportunity—after Owlboy is no more—I'll come up with a much more interesting—"

Sigmund pounced, and the two of them tumbled over on top of each other.

"I hate you!" he shrieked, banging her head on the ground.

Sireena rolled atop her brother, sticking her hand inside his mouth and trying to pull out his tongue.

And it was then that they heard the sound of laughter.

They froze, realizing that they had rolled from the concealing shadows into the light. Humans were watching their fight, pointing and laughing.

An enormously fat human emerged from the crowd, huffing and puffing. Sireena jumped off her brother, looking for her fallen weapon, just as the fat Pinky grabbed them both by the back of their necks, yanking them to their feet.

"Don't make me report you two to the principal," the huge Pinky gurgled. "Apologize to each other and we can all go inside and enjoy the Halloween show."

Sigmund snarled and Sireena did the same in return.

The Pinky shook them both violently. "Apologize!" she shrieked, sounding more terrifying than an angry banshee in search of prey.

"I'm sorry I tried to pull out your tongue," Sireena said to her sibling.

"And I'm sorry I tried to smash your skull in," Sigmund responded in kind.

"Isn't that better?" the gigantic Pinky said. "Now let's all go inside before we miss what's left of the costume show."

And with those words, she hurried her gaggle along, moving toward the front steps of the building.

"That was rather embarrassing," Sireena said.

"I won't tell anybody if you don't."

"Is Owlboy inside?" Sireena asked her brother.

Sigmund tilted his head back and sniffed the air. "Yes, he's there all right."

"Then we should go in," Sireena said, retrieving her weapon from the shadows. "We wouldn't want to miss the end of the show."

Sigmund laughed, picking up his rifle, and the two of them ran for the stairs in full combat mode.

First Owlboy, and then his world, Sireena thought excitedly as they entered the structure, catching sight of one of the human children as it disappeared through a set of double doors.

"He's through there," Sigmund said, motioning toward the doors.

"Then we must be as well," Sireena said, hefting her weapon.

The Sassafras Siblings charged toward the set of double doors. Sigmund threw them open wide as they entered the semidark chamber.

"Where is he?" Sireena spat, the faces of the humans in the large auditorium turning to look at her and her brother. "Where is the accursed Owlboy?"

She waited for their reply, her finger itchy upon the trigger of the weapon that would eliminate the major obstacle preventing them from taking over this world.

Glancing over to see what her brother was doing, Sireena was stunned to see him just standing there, like the idiot he was, staring at the stage.

"What are you doing?" she asked. "You should be scaring them into giving Owlboy up."

Sigmund raised a hand, pointing to the stage. "Look," he said, wearing an expression of shock and awe.

Sireena did as he asked, never expecting to see what she saw before them. "It's impossible," she whispered.

"But it's true," Sigmund responded, a tremble of emotion in his voice.

They started down the aisle of the auditorium toward the stage, their eyes riveted to the ten-foot-tall, green-skinned creature standing upon it.

They had never seen their *mother* look so beautiful.

* * *

Hearing the sudden commotion, Billy wandered out onto the side of the stage to see what was going on.

The audience was buzzing, watching as two monsters, carrying two of the biggest guns he had ever seen, came down the aisle toward the stage.

Billy practically peed himself.

What the heck are the Sassafras Siblings doing here? he wondered, on the verge of panic. The brother and sister ogres were almost at the stage, and were yelling to Randy and Mitchell.

"Mother? Is that you?" Sireena asked. "What are you doing in this horrid place, and how did you free yourself from prison?"

"It was our idea to hunt down Owlboy and conquer this world!" Sigmund yelled, shaking his weapon at the stage. "And we have no intention of sharing!"

This was even more awful than Billy had imagined—the Sassafrasses thought that the Randy/Mitchell beast was their mother.

Man, she musta been a real beauty!

And to make matters worse, they had come up from Monstros to hunt him down and to take over Bradbury.

They certainly are ambitious.

Billy had to do something; he was a superhero, after all.

He ran onstage, and froze, stunned, as the auditorium erupted into applause and laughter.

They think this is part of the show, he realized. He wanted to scream at them that this wasn't a joke, that there were real live monsters in the auditorium and that they should probably take off for the exits—but how seriously would they take a kid in a mutated cow costume?

"Wait!" Sireena Sassafras screamed, coming to the edge of the stage. "This is not our beloved mother."

Sigmund was right beside her. "What do you mean? Of course it is."

Billy ran over to the Randy/Mitchell monster. "You might want to think about getting out of here," he said, leaning close to the monster's belly where he guessed Mitchell's head would be.

Mrs. McKinney was standing at the side of the stage with a big smile on her face, believing that this was all part of Randy and Mitchell's act.

Why isn't anything ever easy? Billy thought as he caught sight of the Sassafras Siblings climbing up on the stage.

"What the heck are you doing, Hooten?" Randy's voice boomed from inside the monster's head. "We got this crowd in the palm of our hand. We're a cinch to win the grand prize. So why don't you go and stand in back with the other dweebs and let the winners show you what a real Halloween costume looks like."

"Yeah, Hooten," said Mitchell Spivey's nasal voice from the belly of the monster.

The long, spindly arms covered with fake hair reached out and pushed Billy backward. Once again the audience burst into laughter as he landed on his butt. Billy struggled to stand in the awkward mutated cow costume, even as Randy and Mitchell were surrounded by the gun-toting Sassafrasses.

"How dare you make fun of the most marvelous mother to ever crawl from the bottomless darkness," Sireena snarled.

"You're right, sister," Sigmund said, leaning in to sniff at the costume. "This *is* an imposter!"

"Who the heck are you two freaks supposed to be?" Randy asked. "If you think those costumes are gonna beat us, you got another think comin'. Let's show 'em what we got, Mitchell."

The Randy/Mitchell monster began to dance around, funky-looking steps equal parts ballet and kung fu.

The crowd went wild as the Sassafras Siblings jumped back, their weapons raised.

In Monstros, Billy would have been able to leap

across the stage and wrestle them to the ground with his super Owlboy strength. But this wasn't Monstros, and he was dressed as a mutated cow.

Not one to admit defeat, Billy launched himself into action, doing the only thing he could think of at the moment to prevent the Sassafrasses from using their weapons on Randy and Mitchell. He grabbed his udder full of fake corrosive fluid, took careful aim and squeezed.

Streams of green goop shot from the tips of the rubber udders and hit the Sassafras Siblings.

"Yeeek!" Sireena screamed. "What is that?"

"It appears to be corrosive material from the udder of a mutated cow," Sigmund replied, feeling the slimy substance between his square fingers.

"Step away from those kids in the monster suit right this instant," Billy commanded in a powerful voice that he hoped would make the Sassafrasses forget that he was dressed like a cow.

No such luck.

Sireena lunged at him, a look of rage on her face. "You've ruined my blouse," she screeched, taking hold of the front of his costume in her large hands.

He was going to threaten to give her another good squirt if she didn't let him go, but he was airborne before the words could leave his mouth.

The audience at the Connery Elementary School Costume Extravaganza went wild with cheers, whistles and applause.

At least they're enjoying themselves, Billy thought as he flew through the air, landing in a heap at the end of the stage.

The Sassafrasses were chasing Randy and Mitchell, and Billy could hear the boys inside the costume screaming as the two ogres began to tear the monster suit to pieces, bellowing at the top of their monstrous lungs that they would not allow their mother to be insulted.

Billy had to do something, but what?

And as if in answer to his prayers, he heard a voice like a squeaky angel calling his name.

"Billy!"

Turning away from the villainy unfolding before him, Billy was shocked to see Victoria standing backstage beside her Big Wheel.

"Hey, Billy," she called out. "Is that a cow suit? You look wicked cute, though I was hopin' you woulda been a fairy princess. What's that thing on your head?"

Billy walked to the edge of the stage. "What are you doing here, Victoria? It's really dangerous right now."

The little girl held up a backpack . . . *his* backpack.

"I saw the bad guys comin' and I thought you might

need your Owlboy suit," the five-year-old said, handing the bag to him.

Billy looked at the costume inside the pack.

Maybe she really is an angel, he mused, ducking in back to make his transformation from mutated cow to . . . Owlboy.

CHAPTER 14

How do all the other super-types do it so fast? Billy wondered, practically breaking his neck as he struggled into his Owlboy costume in the backstage restroom.

He had to keep reminding himself that this was still only Bradbury, and his special abilities were . . . less than special here. He would just have to make do.

Slipping on the goggles, he burst from the bathroom and saw that there was a line. Elementary-school versions of ghosts, witches and spiders danced in front of the door. An especially round ghost pushed him out of the way, darting into the bathroom.

"Gotta go bad!" the ghost moaned.

"Who're you supposed to be?" a little witch asked him.

"I'm Owlboy," Billy said, pushing through the crowd and making his way toward the stage.

"Are you in the show too?" a spider asked, his multiple fake limbs flopping at his side.

"You might say that," Billy said, mentally preparing himself for what he might be seeing as he rounded the corner and exited out onto the stage.

The crowd still seemed to be having a pretty good time, but Mrs. McKinney had grabbed the microphone and was attempting to get them all to settle down.

The Sassafras Siblings had circled Randy and Mitchell, whose costume was now in tatters, and were attempting to use their weapons, but nothing was happening. Billy figured that the guns probably would have worked perfectly fine in Monstros City, but this wasn't Monstros, and different rules applied.

The auditorium broke into thunderous applause as Billy bounded across the stage. He was stunned by their enthusiasm. Suddenly he heard a dog barking wildly, and distracted, looked down at the crowd to see Cole, the owner of the Hero's Hovel Comic Book Shop, and former artist of the old Owlboy comic books before he started having problems with his eyes. His guide dog, Claudius, was sitting beside him in the first row, howling like a werewolf. Then Billy remembered that Cole was one of the judges of the costume contest. The comic book storeowner gave him the thumbs-up, and continued to clap wildly.

Billy resisted the urge to bow, turning to face his foes.

"That's enough of that, Sassafrasses," Billy said in his deepest voice.

The two hideous creatures pointed their weapons at him, and pulled the triggers uselessly.

"Why aren't you destroying him?" Sireena shrieked at her brother.

"I'm trying, but there's no destruction left!" her brother screamed.

Sireena dropped her own weapon and grabbed Sigmund's, viciously slapping him on the side of the head.

"You're just not doing it right!" she roared.

Sireena aimed and fired, and still nothing happened.

"See, see, I told you it was empty!" Sigmund shouted.

The auditorium had grown quiet. Billy got a sense that they thought the show was on the verge of wrapping up.

"Give it up, Sassafrasses," he commanded. "And maybe I'll put in a good word for you and they'll give the two of you a cozy prison cell right next to your mother."

There was the right thing to say in any given situation, and then there was the wrong thing. Billy was always really good about picking the wrong thing.

"Another slight about our most blessed mother!"

Sireena railed, and in a fit of anger she threw her gun at him. The weapon hit Billy square in the chest and knocked him to the floor.

He heard the audience gasp as he tried to catch his breath and crawl out from beneath the extremely heavy gun.

"I don't need any weapons to end your life," Sireena said, lumbering toward him. "I'll do it with my bare hands . . . with pleasure."

This was the part in comic books when the hero usually gathered up his strength, the power of his heroism allowing him to vanquish his foul foe and save the day for the forces of good.

As a sneering Sireena reached for him with claws painted a lovely shade of red, Billy came to the disturbing realization that things weren't looking so hot for the forces of good.

Bored, Victoria had wandered backstage to see if anything more interesting was going on back there.

Kids dressed in costumes were running around like crazy and she almost started to play with them when something even more interesting caught her eye.

High up above the stage, she saw what looked like Santa's sleigh, and maybe even a sack of toys.

Toys, the magic word. She had to get a closer look.

She squeezed her way into a tight area where there were lots of ropes trailing up toward the hanging sleigh. From where she was standing, she could see Billy and the Sassafras Siblings onstage; it looked like they were having fun playing superheroes. It almost made her want to go and join them, but Santa's sleigh called to her.

She couldn't take her eyes off it, imagining what might be inside the magical Christmas ride. Her thoughts were going crazy: why was Santa's sleigh hidden in the back of the auditorium? *Maybe he lives here when he gets tired of the North Pole.*

Curiosity getting the better of her, Victoria studied the ropes. She put her hand on a big knot that was tied around a metal piece sticking out of the wall, and gave it a little tug.

Victoria gasped, surprised at what a little tug could do. The knot began to loosen. She jumped back, bumping into even more ropes. They too started to come undone.

One by one—*thwp! thwp! thwp!*—the ropes shot up into the ceiling, as Santa's sleigh and a whole bunch of other stuff began to slowly swing from side to side.

Maybe Billy was right, she thought as all the things suspended above the stage started to fall.

Maybe I really do have the Destructo Touch.

At first Billy thought the sky was falling.

But then with a burst of strength, he wiggled out from beneath the heavy gun and pushed himself backward.

Just as Sireena made a grab for him, and Santa Claus' sleigh dropped on top of the Sassafrasses' ugly heads in a blizzard of fake snow.

Santa's sleigh? Snow? Billy was tempted to pinch himself to see if he was dreaming. But then he recognized the props from the school's annual holiday pageant. He wondered how in the world the sleigh and fake snow could have come loose, when he saw Victoria sheepishly waving at him from backstage.

"Hey, Billy, watch out for Santa's sleigh!" she yelled.

And it all made perfect sense.

Snow continued to rain down on the stage, but there wasn't a sign of movement from the monsters.

"I've got to get the Sassafras Siblings back to Monstros," Billy yelled to the little girl.

And that was when the crowd in the auditorium went wild.

He'd almost completely forgotten that they were there, watching all the craziness unfold. They were on their feet now, clapping and cheering wildly.

"Bravo! Bravo!" the crowd screamed.

"What are they clapping for?" Victoria asked.

"They think this was all part of the show," Billy said out of the corner of his mouth, bowing for his audience.

"What are they, crazy?" she asked.

Billy's brain was crackling, and an idea—a crazy idea—began to take shape.

"Thank you, folks. Thank you!" Billy said, raising his voice to be heard over the applause and cheers. "And a big hand for all who helped me with this performance," he said, presenting his classmates with a flourish of his hand. "I couldn't have done it without them."

The gang, including Randy and Mitchell, were looking at each other with dumbfounded expressions. They didn't know what the heck had just happened, and Billy didn't have the time to make up anything.

"Get your Big Wheel and wagon," he told Victoria, who had yet to come out on stage for her applause. The little girl ran off as Billy carefully approached the heap of rubble that was the holiday sleigh and several inches of fake snow.

Rummaging through the wreckage, he found the two unconscious monsters. And to more thunderous laughter and applause, he dragged the oblivious Sassafrasses to the edge of the stage.

Darting backstage, he took the pink plastic bike

from his next-door neighbor. "I'm going to borrow this for a little while," he told Victoria, "and you might want to think about getting home before anybody notices you're gone."

"See ya later, alligator!" the little girl said, and was gone in a flash.

Billy rolled the snorting monsters off the edge of the stage to the floor, hopping down to load the Sassafras Siblings onto the back of the Big Wheel's plastic wagon. It was a tight fit, but it would have to do.

He climbed aboard the Big Wheel and started pedaling up the aisle as the families of Connery Elementary school kids cheered him on.

He could still hear them inside the building as he coasted down the handicap ramp and down the driveway of the school to the street, pulling the Sassafrasses in the wagon behind him.

He had to get to Pine Hill Cemetery right away. He had a special delivery for the Monstros City Police.

CHAPTER 15

It was a test to see how strong he really was, Billy was sure of it. If there was some sort of superhero god looking down on him from above, this was most certainly a test to see if he had what it took to be a member of this special, superheroic club.

The Sassafras Siblings each weighed a ton—never mind the fact that he had to pedal all the way from Connery Elementary to the front entrance of Pine Hill Cemetery, which was the farthest entrance from the Sprylock mausoleum, pulling a wagon stuffed full of villainy.

And that was just the beginning.

With his legs feeling like rubber bands, he dragged

the unconscious monsters from the wagon into the mausoleum and dropped them down into the stone coffin.

Billy stood at the bottom of the winding steps, in the darkness of another world, with the still unconscious Sassafrasses at his feet. It was a most excellent bit of luck that the Sassafrasses rolled so well. All he had to do was get them started with a little push, and off they went, tumbling all the way to the bottom.

Flipping open one of the pouches on his utility belt, Billy found the owl-shaped whistle that Archebold had given him during their first meeting.

He brought the whistle to his lips and gave it a powerful blow. The sound of multiple owls all hooting in unison filled the darkness, and a mysterious wind came out of nowhere, pulling eagerly at his costume.

Sireena and Sigmund both began to snort and groan, which meant they were starting to wake up. *Great, that's all I need*, Billy thought, giving the whistle another blow for good measure.

The villains began to twitch, their eyes starting to flutter. Billy was just about to blow on the whistle again when he heard the sound of a motor coming closer.

Archebold emerged from one of the many tunnels wearing a bright yellow helmet and riding on a matching motor scooter.

"What's up, boss man?" he asked, pulling up alongside him.

"I was wondering what I should do with these two," Billy said, pointing at the Sassafras Siblings. They seemed to have regained consciousness and were now sitting up, their bulging and bloodshot eyes attempting to focus.

"Sweet serpents' saliva!" Archebold exclaimed. "Those are the Sassafras Siblings!"

"No kiddin'," Billy said. "They came looking for me and attacked my Halloween costume extravaganza."

"Oh dear," the goblin gasped, his stubby fingers going to his mouth. "Did anybody see them . . . I mean, anybody of the human persuasion?"

Billy nodded. "Oh yeah, they were seen all right. They got taken out onstage in front of at least two hundred assorted family and friends."

"Ouch!" Archebold said, his face screwing up in imaginary pain.

"I can just imagine the damage control for this one. At least I've got a good imagination," Billy said. "And speaking of damage control, is it all right to leave these guys here with you so I can get back and see how much trouble I'm going to be in?"

Archebold reached into his tuxedo jacket pocket and produced an enormous walkie-talkie. "Come in,

Fleabag, this is Gorgeous Goblin, do you copy? Come in, Fleabag, come in. This is Gorgeous . . ."

Halifax suddenly stepped from the shadows in front of Billy and Archebold, both of them screaming at the same time.

"There you are," Archebold said, his hand clenched to his chest. "You just about gave me a heart attack."

"Why is my code name Fleabag?" the troll asked, casually scratching at the large tuft of fur that hung from his hairy armpit.

"Never mind that," Archebold said. "We're going to need a transport cage so we can get these vile villains over to Chief Bloodwart and . . ."

The troll was suddenly gone and the sound of enormous footfalls filled the darkness.

"What the heck?" Billy yelled over the booming step.

It was before them suddenly—a gigantic robot, what little source of light there was in the darkness of the tunnels reflecting off its metal surface.

Billy didn't know what to think. Were the Sassafrasses about to be rescued by a faithful member of their gang or another villain looking to team up with the motley pair? *Stuff like that happens all the time in comics.*

But then Billy realized that there was something

oddly familiar about the giant machine. And then he noticed that the giant robot was carrying a transport cage, and it all became clear.

"We are saved, Brother!" Sireena slurred, trying to get to her feet but falling back down on her ample butt. "I feel like I've been rolled down a flight of stone steps," she muttered, again trying to stand.

"Who is our mysterious saviour?" Sigmund asked, not even bothering to try to stand. "The Ghostly Gang, perhaps, or maybe even Dr. Sticky—he was always fascinated by mechanical men."

Two blasts of steam erupted from the vents on either side of the mechanical man's head, and its eyes glowed a fiery red.

"Don't get your hopes up," Billy said to the brother and sister as he approached the robot.

"Careful, sir," Archebold warned, grabbing his arm.

"It's all right," Billy answered. "I know who it is."

There was a whirring of gears as the robot's head flipped backward to reveal Halifax. "I would've been here sooner but I had a hard time getting the Death-Bot 180 through the front door."

"So this is the 180 model, eh?" Billy asked, admiring the robotic suit.

"It's not as cool as the 390, but it'll do in a pinch," Halifax said. "Now if you'll excuse me, I have some trash to pick up."

And with those words the three-fingered, clawlike hands of the robot suit released the cage, sending it crashing to the floor. There was a soft pinging sound as a green light on top of the cage began to flash, and the barred door slid up.

"Quickly, we must escape to the shadow paths," Sireena slurred, managing to get to her feet but lurching to the side as one of her high heels flew off.

Sigmund just rolled around on the ground like a bloated slug.

Halifax walked the robot body over to the Sassafrasses and picked them up, one in each clawed hand. They kicked and screamed as they were being hauled to the open cage and unceremoniously dropped inside.

"Mark my words, Owlboy," Sireena scowled as the door slid down. "We will find a way to destroy you."

"What she said," Sigmund echoed haughtily as he peered through the metal bars.

"You guys might be outta luck on that one," Billy said, turning to his friends. "If what I suspect is waiting for me back home, there won't be much of me left to destroy."

Halifax clumped over to the transport cage and picked it up as if it weighed nothing. "Next stop, Monstros City police headquarters," he announced.

"Do you think we'll end up in Beelzebub Prison, Sister?" Billy heard Sigmund ask.

"Most likely," Sireena replied with venom.

"Oh, good. Do you think Mother will be glad to see us?" he asked with sincerity.

"She'll be thrilled, brother dear," Sireena answered. "Absolutely thrilled."

And then they were gone, the sound of the Death-Bot 180's heavy metal footsteps swallowed by the darkness.

Billy turned to Archebold. "So I guess I'll see ya later then."

The goblin was climbing back onto his scooter. "Maybe it won't be so bad."

Billy shrugged. "Guess I won't know till I get back."

"Guess not," Archebold agreed.

"Nice knowing you," Billy said, putting out a gloved hand.

"Same here," Archebold said, pumping Billy's hand up and down.

Billy turned, slowly walking back toward the stone steps that would bring him up to the surface as if he were heading for his execution.

They've probably figured out by now that it was all real, Billy thought, pedaling Victoria's Big Wheel back to school. In his mind he conjured up images of the police and maybe even the United States Army all parked in front of the school, ready to defend the people of Bradbury against any more monster threats.

He imagined the citizens of Bradbury running around with flaming torches in search of monsters like the villagers always did in the old Frankenstein movies.

Not good, not good at all.

And to make matters worse, he was going to have to explain himself to his parents.

"Mom, Dad, it's true—I am a superhero." And of course his mother would start crying, and Dad would drop to his knees, shaking his fists at the heavens.

"Why, why has my only son been burdened with this great responsibility? Why him, why?"

Billy glanced at the watch beneath his left glove. He hadn't been gone all that long. *The whole Monstros time thing again.* He was getting closer now, and his stomach felt like it was tied in knots—not just a couple of knots, about a few hundred of them.

At first he wasn't sure, but then he was certain. Billy could hear the low buzzing of voices all talking together, the sound that you got when a good-sized crowd had gathered.

Driving past the high hedges that surrounded the outskirts of the school, he reached the driveway and brought the Big Wheel to a stop.

"Oh. My. God," Billy said, staring through his Owl-boy goggles to the end of the driveway and to the front of the school. They were all still here, every one of the families and all their kids.

And he could just imagine what they were saying.

"Those were real monsters, I tell you! Somebody better call the police . . . and maybe even the army!"

"It was that Hooten kid for sure . . . my son always said there was something wrong with him!"

"Our Halloween costume extravaganza was ruined. I say we cancel Halloween . . . and maybe even Christmas!"

Billy couldn't allow them to cancel Christmas. He pedaled up the driveway to face the angry mob. Maybe there was something he could say to convince them things weren't so bad, that things might have gotten a little messy, but he had handled it.

Owlboy had handled it just fine.

"Yeah, that's gonna fly," he muttered, bringing the Big Wheel to a stop at the curb. The first members of the angry mob noticed him.

"Hey, it's the kid in the superhero suit!" said somebody from the crowd.

"He's gonna get it for sure," said another.

Billy felt his world start to crumble. He was gonna get it for sure; truer words were never spoken.

"Hey, everybody," he said, waving to the crowd. He

was trying to be upbeat, and hoped that maybe this would translate to the crowd. "Nothing to worry about here. Everything is fine. I handled it."

"You handled it, all right," somebody yelled, and then the crowd started to laugh.

Laugh? Shouldn't they be lighting torches and screaming for my blood? Billy thought.

Mr. and Mrs. Hooten pushed through the crowd toward him and Billy prepared for what was sure to be a bloody onslaught.

"I can explain everything," he began, certain that he had used the exact phrasing at least a hundred times before when he felt as though he was about to be in really big trouble.

"Don't worry about it," his mom said with a wave of her hand. "I thought what you did with the cow suit was very imaginative."

"Cow suit?" Billy questioned. "But that's not what I . . ."

Dad spoke up next, looking really excited. "Yeah, the whole monster cow thing was cool, but when you came out as the superhero guy, that was classic."

"Yeah . . . wasn't it?" Billy said, and giggled nervously.

The crowd had moved toward him, full of smiles.

"That was the best Halloween pageant I ever saw," said Michelle O'Neil's father. "They're usually way more boring than that."

"When those two monsters with the guns came in, I just about jumped out of my seat!" said Mrs. Gablonsky, a baby sound asleep on her shoulder. "Who would have thought you kids could put on such a show?"

Mrs. Hooten bent down and gave Billy a big hug, embarrassing the crap out of him. "I can't believe you were able to keep all this secret. You and your little friends are so creative."

The crowd parted, allowing Mrs. McKinney, holding onto the shoulders of Randy and Mitchell, to come through. "I just wish they had cleared some of these things with me first," she said sternly, but Billy could see a smile forming at the corners of her wrinkled mouth. "However, for something so thoroughly entertaining, I suppose I'll let it slide this time."

The crowd was laughing and clapping again as Billy locked eyes with his mortal enemies. Randy was wearing the top half of the elaborate monster suit, his ugly face sticking out from the beast's now permanently open maw. Mitchell was still wearing the lower half, his normally weasely upper body morphing into the bottom of some hideous monstrosity.

They both looked as though they were in shock, and in their gaze Billy could see that they were looking for answers from him. Answers that he wasn't about to give.

"Yeah, I thought we'd do things a little differently

this year," Billy said, laying it on thick. "Give everybody a little more bang for their buck."

Randy and Mitchell just stared.

Over to the side Billy caught a glimpse of his costumed pals and gave them a wink.

"Gotta hand it to you, Hooten," Dwight the Grim Reaper yelled. "You really pulled this one off big-time."

"You are the Halloween costume extravaganza master!" Kathy B, in her witch costume, yelled, giving him the thumbs-up. "Good job, Billy!"

"Yeah, good job," Danny said, flapping his cilia arms in what Billy thought might've been some sort of paramecium salute.

Reggie waved a handful of paper towel and toilet paper rolls that had come off his Transmogrifier costume, as even more of the colored tubes fell to the ground. "Who did you get to play the two monsters, Bill?" he asked. "They were great."

Billy was momentarily stumped. He wasn't about to tell them that they were real monsters that were out to erase him from the blackboard of existence, but he had to say something.

"Oh, they were just a couple guys I met in acting class . . . yeah, that's it," he said, amazed that he could come up with such a great fib. He had actually attended acting classes last year over summer vacation, and had made some new friends there. He hadn't talked to any of them since classes ended in July, but what his school pals didn't know wouldn't hurt them. "They had to get going, but wanted me to tell you guys how much fun they had."

Again the crowd began to clap. How much crazier did it have to be in Bradbury before people actually took notice?

A dog's steady bark filled the air and Billy saw that Mrs. McKinney had found Cole and his guide dog, Claudius, and was herding them to the front of the crowd. "Mr. Cole has something to say."

Cole cleared his throat loudly, a signal for the crowd to quiet down so he could speak. Claudius helped with a booming bark and then sat down at his master's feet, looking up at him lovingly.

"First of all, I'd like to thank everybody for inviting me to be a judge at your special function this evening." The large man smiled, looking around at everybody, his eyes grotesquely huge behind the lenses of his thick glasses. "At first I thought it was going to be pretty boring, and I expected to fall asleep after the fiftieth astronaut or the seventy-seventh fairy princess."

He paused for effect.

"Boy, was I wrong! And even though this was the

first Halloween pageant I was ever invited to attend, I can't imagine a more exciting one."

The crowd broke into applause, and once again Billy wondered if this was all some kind of crazy dream. He reached down and gave his leg a little pinch through the heavy material of his Owlboy costume. It hurt like heck, and he didn't wake up. And that just proved that no matter how bizarre this all seemed, it was real.

Cole went on.

"I was supposed to pick a single winner for the costume contest," he said, reaching into the front pocket of his fancy Hawaiian shirt. This one was adorned with big-headed tiki statues and flaming torches. "A single winner to get this." He showed the crowd the hundred-dollar gift certificate to his store.

Billy gasped at the sight of it.

"But after such a show, I realize that I can't give this to just one person." Again with the dramatic pause. "So I've decided to give each of you—Billy, Randy and Mitchell—a one-hundred-dollar gift certificate to the Hero's Hovel. And superspecial discounts to all the students at Connery Elementary, since you all did such a fantastic job."

The crowd whooped and cheered. Ghosts, ghouls, witches, robots and even parameciums clapped enthusiastically.

And if by some strange chance this was actually a dream, please, please, please make it so I never wake up, Billy thought excitedly as he accepted his prize.

Randy and Mitchell still wore the same stunned expressions on their faces as they took their prizes.

A guy with a camera approached them. "I'm from the *Bradbury Daily Journal* and was wondering if I could get a picture."

Billy approached his mortal enemies, not wanting to get too close. Cole loomed above them, smiling for the picture.

"Hold up your prizes, kids," the man from the newspaper said as he raised his camera.

Billy did as he was told, as did the others, and just as the camera flashed, freezing their moment of victory, Randy spoke, saying the first words to him since their dealings with the Sassafras Siblings up on stage.

"Those were *real* monsters, weren't they, Hooten?" Randy said, his head slowly turning to look at him intensely.

The photographer wanted another shot. Billy put on his biggest smile.

"What're you, crazy, Randy?" he said as the flash went off, temporarily blinding them in an explosion of white.

"There's no such thing as monsters."

*   *   *

It's been a long night, a really long night, Billy thought as his parents' car finally pulled into the driveway of his house. He was looking forward to getting out of his costume and hopping right into bed. It was tiring work being a superhero, and a Halloween costume extravaganza winner.

Billy got out of the car and remembered that he still had something to do. Trudging his tired body around to the back of the car, he pulled Victoria's Big Wheel from the trunk and set it down on the driveway.

"That was very nice of Victoria to let you borrow her bike for your show," his mother said, following his father up onto the porch.

"Yeah," he said. "She's quite a gal, that Victoria is." Images of demolished sections of Monstros City filled his head. "Quite a gal."

"Are you coming up?" his mother asked.

"I just want to put this back in the McDevitts' yard and I'll be in," he said.

His mother was going into the house when she stopped and turned in the doorway. "Hey, Billy," she called as he was starting to pedal the pink three-wheeled bike across the yard.

"Yeah, Mom?"

"Good job tonight," she said. "It was really something special."

Billy smiled. If only she knew the half of it. If he had failed, the Sassafrasses would likely have taken over all of Bradbury by now.

"Thanks," he said, pleased that she'd had a good time—and that he was able to thwart the insidious plans of the evil siblings.

She gave him another one of her proud smiles, the kind that always made him feel that he was something more than just a weird little kid, and went into the house, closing the door behind her.

He was trying to be extra quiet as he left his driveway and started across the thick patch of grass that separated the two properties. His plan was to leave the Big Wheel in the McDevitts' yard and then dash right back to his own house.

Nobody would know he'd even been there.

A window on the second floor of the McDevitt house came open.

"You better not have busted it," Victoria's voice called out.

Nabbed.

"It's fine," Billy said in a whisper.

"Where are the Sassafras Siblings?" she asked. "Did you take them home?"

"Yeah, Archebold and Halifax are making sure they get back to their mommy."

"That's good," the little girl said. "I came right back here when you left so my mommy wouldn't worry."

"Did she know you were out?"

"Nope," the little girl said proudly. "I'm Ninja Girl, don't you remember?"

Billy nodded. "Of course you are. How could I forget?"

The cold night wind started to blow, carrying with it the smoky smell of autumn, and swarms of leaves skittered and crackled across the ground like some kind of weird Halloween bugs.

Billy suddenly realized how tired he was.

Man, I don't even know how I'm still standing.

"Okay, put a fork in me, I'm done," he said to the little girl in the window. "Time to go to bed. See ya later."

He had started across the grass divider when Victoria called out to him.

"Hey, Billy."

"Yeah," he answered from his driveway.

"I don't want to be Ninja Girl no more," she told him.

"Okay," he answered, too exhausted to ask why she wanted to give up the title.

"I want to be Owlgirl," she said. Billy froze halfway up his porch steps.

"Can I be Owlgirl, Billy?"

He didn't have the strength to deal with this right then. "Why don't we talk about it tomorrow?" he said, buying himself some time.

"Okeydoke, see ya tomorrow, Owlboy!" Victoria said, closing the window.

Opening the back door, Billy hoped that by the time tomorrow rolled around, she would have forgotten all about wanting to be his sidekick.

And maybe he'd be six feet tall when he woke up, and it would be Christmas, and his parents would have bought him his very own Komodo dragon.

"Yeah, right," he said aloud, closing the door and leaving the night outside.

He couldn't be so lucky.

Acknowledgments

As always, many thanks to my loving wife, LeeAnne, and Mulder the Wonderdog, for allowing me to live in their house.

Special thanks to Stephanie Lane for understanding what the heck I was talking about; to Liesa Abrams for backing me up; and to Eric Powell for really bringing Billy and the world of Monstros to life.

Thanks also to Christopher Golden, Mike & Christine Mignola, Dave "Shiny" Kraus, John & Jana, Darth Harry & Grand Moff Hugo, Don Kramer, Greg Skopis, James "the Pump" Mignogna, Mom & Dad Sniegoski, David Carroll, Ken Curtis, Mom & Dad Fogg, Lisa Clancy, Zach Howard, Kim & Abby, Jon & Flo, Pat & Bob, Pete Donaldson, Jay Sanders, Timothy Cole, and they who walk in shadows down at Cole's Comics in Lynn, Massachusetts.

The adventure continues.

THOMAS E. SNIEGOSKI is a novelist and comic book scripter who has worked for every major company in the comics industry.

As a comic book writer, his work includes *Stupid, Stupid Rat Tails*, a miniseries prequel to the international hit *Bone*. He has also written tales featuring such characters as Hellboy, Batman, Daredevil, Wolverine, and the Punisher.

He is also the author of the groundbreaking quartet of teen fantasy novels entitled The Fallen, the first of which (*Fallen*) has been produced as a television movie for the ABC Family Channel. The two books in his Sleeper Conspiracy, a new series, *Sleeper Code* and *Sleeper Agenda*, have recently been released. With Christopher Golden, he is the coauthor of the dark fantasy series The Menagerie, as well as the young readers' fantasy series OutCast, recently optioned by Universal Pictures. Sniegoski and Golden also wrote the graphic novel *BPRD: Hollow Earth*, a spinoff of the fan favorite comic book series Hellboy.

Sniegoski was born and raised in Massachusetts, where he still lives with his wife, LeeAnne, and their Labrador retriever, Mulder. Please visit the author at www.sniegoski.com.

ERIC POWELL is the writer and artist of the award-winning comic book series The Goon for Dark Horse Comics. He has also contributed work to such comic titles as *Arkham Asylum*, *Buffy the Vampire Slayer*, *Hellboy: Weird Tales*, *Star Wars Tales*, *The Incredible Hulk*, *MAD Magazine*, *Swamp Thing*, and *The Simpsons*.